"No spell books in here," Paige commented. "No crystals, candles, or sacrificial knives, either." It was just the normal closet of a normal guy. She did a quick check of the shoe rack and the tie caddy. Nothing.

The bathroom cabinet was filled with the usual assortment of pain medications and toiletries. No potion bottles or vials of blood or whatever else evil people kept in their medicine chests.

"What is your deal, Daniel?" Paige asked as she headed back toward the living room. "Could you really be just a cute control freak who talks to his friends about how to impress Phoebe?"

She wandered over toward a huge aquarium built into the wall behind the couch. A giant, bright orange fish with horns growing from its head swam lazily around the corals inside. Paige tapped on the glass and the fish came toward her, so she bent down to take a closer look. It was gorgeous. But it wasn't a clue to any evil behavior on Daniel's part.

She straightened up with a sigh—and found herself gazing into the glowing yellow eyes of a demon.

Paige froze. The demon was reflected in the glass of the aquarium. It stood behind her, looking over her shoulder.

She spun around, automatically raising her arm to throw a fireball.

Charmed®

Published by Simon & Schuster

SWEET TALKIN' DEMON

An original novel by Laura J. Burns

Based on the hit TV series created by

Constance M. Burge

SIMON SPOTLIGHT ENTERTAINMENT
New York   London   Toronto   Sydney

This book is a work of fiction. Any references to historical events, real people, or real locales are used fictitiously. Other names, characters, places, and incidents are the product of the author's imagination, and any resemblance to actual events or locales or persons, living or dead, is entirely coincidental.

S|S|E

SIMON SPOTLIGHT ENTERTAINMENT
An imprint of Simon & Schuster Children's Publishing Division
1230 Avenue of the Americas, New York, New York 10020
® and © 2006 Spelling Television Inc. All Rights Reserved.
All rights reserved, including the right of reproduction in whole or in part in any form.
SIMON SPOTLIGHT ENTERTAINMENT and related logo are trademarks of Simon & Schuster, Inc.
Manufactured in the United States of America
10 9 8 7 6 5 4 3
Library of Congress Control Number 2006923043
ISBN-13: 978-1-4169-1469-3
ISBN-10: 1-4169-1469-2

Chapter 1

"Wow. You are one hot mama," Phoebe Halliwell said, stopping in the kitchen doorway of her Victorian house. Her older sister, Piper, was wearing a slinky black cocktail dress and high stiletto heels. Her long dark hair had been pulled up into a chic French twist. And she was bouncing her baby, Wyatt, on one hip.

"Thanks. I'm hoping to escape without spit-up on my dress," Piper joked. "You look pretty hot yourself."

Phoebe spun around to show off the full skirt of her dark pink gown. "Do you think it's too much for a charity ball?" she asked. "I could change."

"Again?" Their half sister, Paige Matthews, bustled into the room and snatched Wyatt from Piper's arms. "You've already gone through four outfits." She made a funny face at the baby and began to dance him around the kitchen.

"It's a museum fund-raiser. There will be

press there," Phoebe pointed out. "I have to look stunning."

Piper raised one eyebrow, her patented skeptical look.

"I'm representing the paper," Phoebe told her. "I have to look my best in order to make the *Bay Mirror* look its best."

"Oh, please." Paige chuckled. "You change your clothes four times before you even go to work in the morning."

"Same thing," Phoebe said. "I'm still looking good for the paper!" She'd been working as an advice columnist at the San Francisco newspaper for a while now, and she saw it as her duty to be as fashionable as possible. After all, who wanted romantic advice from somebody who looked as if they couldn't land a date?

"Wyatt napped earlier, so he should be awake for at least a few hours," Piper told Paige. "Thank you so much for babysitting. I know it's no fun for you to stay in on a Saturday night."

"Are you kidding? Wyatt's the cutest guy I've spent a Saturday with in ages," Paige cracked. "Besides, it's a big day for you and Leo. Anniversaries only come once a year!"

"Where is Leo, by the way?" Phoebe asked. "You're all ready to go and he's not even home."

Piper frowned and brushed some lint off her dress. "I know. He should have been here an hour ago. He's always late these days."

"Working overtime at the Whitelighter business?" Phoebe guessed. Piper's husband was a Whitelighter, which meant he was charged with protecting witches—like Piper, Phoebe, and Paige. Of course, he was more than just a Whitelighter to them. And the three sisters didn't need all that much protecting these days. They were pretty much the most powerful witches around when they combined their powers. Together, they had the Power of Three, which made them a force to be reckoned with. Many of Leo's other charges needed him a lot more often than they did.

"I don't know why he's been so swamped lately," Piper complained. "There's no big evil happening, at least as far as we know. So why are all his charges in trouble so much?"

"Don't worry, he'll be here," Paige said. "It's your anniversary. You're the love of his life. Do the math."

Piper nodded. "Ever since I had Wyatt, I feel like all the excitement has vanished from my relationship with Leo. We're so busy worrying and scheduling and playing with the baby—not to mention changing his diapers—that we haven't had much time for each other. We really need a nice, romantic dinner to get us back on track."

A swirl of light filled the room, and Leo appeared. His blond hair was a mess, and his green eyes were filled with anxiety. Phoebe felt a stab of worry. Her brother-in-law looked terrible.

"You look terrible," Paige told him.

"Thanks," he said sarcastically, glancing at her. He mustered up a smile for Wyatt, then turned to Piper.

"Our reservation is in twenty minutes and you're still not even dressed," she told him. "You'd better orb upstairs—I don't think you have time to walk."

Leo grimaced. "I'm sorry, honey," he said. "I can't go."

Uh-oh, Phoebe thought. She shot a look at Paige, and the two of them began inching toward the kitchen door. This was not a conversation they wanted to be part of.

"I'm sorry?" Piper asked in a chilly voice. "You can't go where? I know you're not talking about our anniversary dinner, because canceling that isn't an option."

"Piper, I feel terrible," Leo said. "But I've got a charge in real trouble—"

"And you have an anniversary once a year," Piper interrupted. "Why can't someone else take care of your charge for this one night?"

"Because Kerria is *my* charge," Leo replied. "I wouldn't feel right just abandoning her."

Paige made a face and bolted from the room with Wyatt. Phoebe followed as quickly as she could. Piper was not going to be happy with that last comment, and they both knew it.

"But you can just abandon your wife?" Piper's voice reached Phoebe as she fled. Then she was out in the foyer and away from the blowup she knew was coming.

Paige was hiding out in the living room. "Well, that's not pretty," she said as Phoebe entered the room. "I can't believe Leo is bailing on their anniversary."

"It must be something serious," Phoebe said. "Otherwise he would never risk the wrath of Piper like this."

"She has a point, though," Paige replied. "He could ask another Whitelighter to cover for him. Or ask the Elders to assign someone else. I'd do it, but I've got to watch Wyatt." Paige was half-Whitelighter and half-witch, so she always tried to see both sides of the question.

"And I'd do it, but I'll get fired if I don't go to this event." Phoebe sighed. "Poor Piper. She got all dolled up and everything, too. That's the worst."

"What is?" Piper asked, storming into the living room. "Being stood up by your husband, or having him orb away right in the middle of an argument?"

"Yeesh." Phoebe winced. "He really just orbed away?"

"While I was in the middle of a sentence," Piper said. "Can you believe that? It's just . . . just . . ."

"Rude?" Phoebe put in.

"Inconsiderate?" Paige suggested.

Piper looked back and forth between them. "I

was going to say hurtful." She dropped down onto the couch, her expression miserable. "He doesn't even care about our anniversary. Our relationship must be in worse shape than I thought."

Phoebe sat down next to her. "Don't even think that way," she said. "Of course Leo cares. He's just frantic over whatever is happening with his charge. Just wait—he'll come home tonight with three dozen roses and spend the rest of the week apologizing to you."

"Great," Piper said. "And in the meantime I'll spend my anniversary alone."

"Well, Wyatt and I will try to show you a good time," Paige said. "We have a big night of peekaboo planned."

"No way. You're not wasting that killer outfit," Phoebe declared. "You're coming with me to the museum fund-raiser."

Piper stared at her in surprise.

"What? I don't have a date," Phoebe said. "As usual. And you're already dressed for it. So come with me. Please? I'll feel less like a loser."

"You're not a loser," Piper told her. "You're just in a dating slump."

"A two-month-long dating slump. I think that counts as a dating drought," Phoebe said. "So I refuse to feel sorry for you because your husband is busy. At least you have somebody to kiss good night."

"Not lately," Piper mumbled.

"That's it. You're definitely going with Phoebe," Paige declared. "You could use a fun night out. Otherwise you're just going to sit around here and think about Leo."

Piper bit her lip. "It *has* been a while since I went out and blew off some steam."

"And you've got a babysitter all lined up," Paige said.

Phoebe jumped to her feet and held out her hand to Piper. "Let's go, sister. We're gonna party!"

"Didn't I tell you this party would be great?" Phoebe said an hour later. "Check out that ice sculpture!" She squinted at the life-size reproduction of a Matisse nude done in clear, cold ice.

"I'm more interested in the hors d'oeuvres," Piper replied. "They're amazing. I wonder who the chef is?"

Phoebe smiled to herself. Piper had been a chef before she began running the nightclub they owned, P3. The fact that she was taking a professional interest in the museum gala was a good sign that she was starting to get over being stood up by Leo. Phoebe's cheering-up plan was working! Not only that, but the fund-raising gala was hopping. The gorgeous atrium lobby of the San Francisco Museum of Modern Art was decorated to perfection, champagne was flowing, and Phoebe had already spotted at least three celebrities in the crowd of well-dressed partyers.

"Ask Phoebe!" called a blond girl with a ponytail and a huge camera. "Smile!"

Phoebe spun Piper to face the camera and put on a big grin while the photographer snapped the picture.

"What was that all about?" Piper asked.

"Are you kidding? A shindig like this will definitely make the society page," Phoebe said. "And maybe we'll be there, smiling at the adoring public."

Piper snorted. "I thought this was supposed to be for charity, not for publicity."

"It is," Phoebe told her. "The museum is opening a new wing devoted to emerging artists from third world countries. But having a big, fancy party like this means they get lots of rich people to come, and the rich people give lots of money to help the artists."

"And *we're* here . . . why?" Piper asked.

"Oh, the paper always contributes to the museum funds. I just lucked into the gala tickets because my boss is away this week," Phoebe said. "Usually she goes to these things."

A loud thumping sound echoed through the space as the string quartet stopped playing. A tall, thin guy with blond hair tapped on the microphone, sending another *thump* through the air.

"Ouch!" Phoebe cried. "Turn it down!" A few people nearby covered their ears to block out the obnoxious screeching noise of the mike. Phoebe wondered who the guy was—hadn't he ever used a microphone before?

"I guess it's on," the blond guy said with a wry smile. "Sorry about that. I'm not used to public speaking."

Everybody laughed, and Phoebe found herself laughing right along with them. This dude was cute!

"My name is Daniel Lemond, and I'm one of the organizers of tonight's event," the guy went on. "On behalf of the San Francisco Museum of Modern Art, I'd like to thank you for coming to our little get-together. Without the support of people like yourselves, we wouldn't be able to undertake such an ambitious project."

"Who is *he*?" Piper murmured. "He's so good-looking, you'd think the museum would put him on all their brochures and stuff."

Phoebe laughed. She hadn't noticed Daniel in the crowd, but as he went on to describe the emerging artists project, she couldn't take her eyes off him. "Wow. He's really into this program," she whispered to Piper. "He's practically glowing just talking about it!"

"I'd like to bring out the very first artist sponsored by the museum," Daniel said. "She's been doing amazing work with sculpture in her native Cambodia. Give a warm welcome to Sovann Duong."

Phoebe and Piper clapped along with the rest of the crowd as a pretty young woman stepped up to the mike and spoke a few words in halting English. The museum curator came next, explaining exactly how the new program was going to work.

"Let's go," Piper said, tugging on Phoebe's arm.

"Huh? Where?" Phoebe asked. "You want to leave already?"

"No, I want you to go talk to that guy," Piper told her. "You know you want to."

"What guy?" Phoebe asked, but she could feel a giant grin working its way across her face. She'd been watching Daniel Lemond ever since he left the microphone. He was standing off to one side of the podium, fiddling with the bow tie of his tux. He was adorable.

"The one who cares about third world artists and also knows how to organize a kick-ass party like this," Piper said. "And the one you've been staring at for the past ten minutes."

"I don't know. Do you think it's tacky to hit on a guy at a charity ball?" Phoebe asked. "I mean, he's probably just a professional event planner doing his job."

"So what?" Piper asked. "Would you think it was tacky if a guy hit on you at work?"

"No. I'd think it was weird that some stranger was sitting in my office, watching me type," Phoebe cracked.

"Just go say hi," Piper told her. "Please. Somebody should have romance in their life, and it obviously isn't me these days."

Phoebe rubbed her sister's shoulder. "I'm sorry about Leo."

"I don't want to talk about it," Piper said. "I want to live vicariously through you. So go tell hot Mr. Daniel Lemond that you're loving this party he threw."

"Okay." Phoebe combed her hair with her fingers and put on a smile. "Hot Mr. Daniel Lemond, you don't know what's about to hit you!"

"Here comes the choo-choo," Paige said in a singsong voice. She swung the little plastic spoon through the air, making it jerk back and forth like a train as she aimed at Wyatt's mouth. "Into the tunnel!"

She expected him to open up and let her feed him.

Instead, he opened up—and sneezed all over the spoonful of baby food. Then he burst into tears.

"Wow." Paige sat back and stared at her nephew. "I didn't think a sneeze was *that* upsetting." Although, now that she thought about it, Wyatt had been sneezing a lot tonight. And ever since Piper and Phoebe left for the museum gala, the baby had been cranky. She'd assumed it was just because he missed his mother, but suddenly she wasn't so sure.

"Let's take a break from din-din, okay?" she said. She took Wyatt out of his high chair and sat him on her lap, bouncing him up and down a bit to make him stop crying. But even when his screams quieted down, he kept sniffling. His little face was all red, and he kept rubbing his eyes.

"You look like I feel after a really bad night of demon fighting," Paige joked. "Or after a really fun night at a party."

Wyatt gazed back at her with big, sad eyes.

"I know you can't talk yet," Paige said. "But you're an excellent communicator, baby. You're feeling sick, aren't you?"

Wyatt sneezed. Then he sneezed again. And then he began to cough.

"Oh, poor thing." Paige hugged him close. "You've got a cold. And it sounds seriously nasty."

Wyatt squirmed in her arms, trying to get away. But when she loosened them, he started to cry again. The poor kid didn't know what he wanted. Paige understood just how he felt— whenever *she* had a cold, nothing helped her feel better either.

"I wish I could help you," she told him. "Maybe some echinacea . . ." Her voice trailed off as a new idea hit her. Echinacea was an herb, right? They had plenty of herbs here in Halliwell Manor—because herbs were used in potions to do all kinds of magic. So in a way, a magic potion was just a big herbal milk shake. And why not give one to little Wyatt?

She stared at him, thinking about it. One of

the most important rules of being a witch was not to use magic for personal gain. But making a potion to vanquish a cold that somebody else had didn't count as personal gain. Did it? And if she were going to make a potion, she might as well write up a cold-vanquishing spell to go along with it.

"Wyatt, you just sit tight," she said, lifting him back into his high chair. "I'm gonna make it all better!"

She dashed over to the cabinets and began grabbing bottles and envelopes full of herbs. Making potions was one of her favorite Wiccan things, and she'd been working to perfect her skills ever since she'd discovered her witchy heritage a couple of years ago. "We'll start with sage, obviously—everybody knows that's good for colds. And then I'm going to boil some mugwort to keep you from getting a sore throat, and chamomile flowers to reduce swelling in your poor little sinuses. Oh, and red clover for your cough. And echinacea, of course."

Wyatt just sneezed in response.

Paige kept an eye on him as she mixed up the potion, and by the time she was finished, he was asleep in his high chair. *I guess I'll have to whisper the spell*, she thought. She tiptoed over to Wyatt, then glanced down at the bottle of potion in her hand. Since all the herbs were medicinal, she could put them in a bottle and feed them to the baby. But it was a vanquishing potion, after all.

And when she and her sisters vanquished demons, they threw the potion at the demon.

Could she really hurl a vanquishing potion at Wyatt?

He coughed in his sleep.

The poor thing feels miserable, Paige told herself. *That cold might as well be a demon!* She threw the potion down on the tray of the high chair, so that it broke and swirled up and over Wyatt. As it did, she quickly said her spell: "Sickness like an evil, loosen your bond. Vanquished are you. Be gone!"

Wyatt started awake, blinking in surprise. Paige gazed back at him, waiting for a wail or a cough or a sneeze. But he just sat there, his blue eyes clear and his sniffles gone.

"How do you feel, big boy?" Paige asked.

Wyatt grabbed for the jar of baby food on the table, his pudgy little hands working hard to get at it. Paige chuckled. Hungry was a good sign. He wasn't fussy or whiny . . . or sick at all. The potion and the spell had worked!

She pulled up a chair and sat back down to feed Wyatt again. He immediately ate the first spoonful and smiled at Paige. She grinned back. "Who needs medical school when you've got magic?" she asked.

"Thank you so much for coming," Daniel Lemond said as the museum gala swirled around him. "You've really helped make this event a success."

The little old lady wearing a blond bouffant

wig smiled and patted his hand. "You're a good boy," she told him.

"Um . . . thank you," Daniel stammered, trying to pull his hand away. The little old lady held tight, still gazing up at him with shining eyes.

Phoebe had been watching him with the elderly woman for the past five minutes, and she stifled a laugh. Cute, polite Daniel was no match for a determined octogenarian. He obviously needed rescuing.

"Excuse me," she said, stepping up next to the old lady.

The lady ignored her.

"Excuse me!" Phoebe yelled into her ear. This time the woman jumped and turned toward her.

"Hi. I need to steal Daniel for a few minutes," Phoebe said loudly. "There's been an emergency with the dessert trays."

"Can't you handle it, dear?" the little old lady asked. "I was so enjoying talking to Danny here. He's a good boy."

Phoebe shot a glance at Daniel. His eyes were wide, and he looked almost afraid. "He certainly is," she replied. "And that's why he's the only one who can solve the dessert crisis."

The lady frowned and reluctantly let go of Daniel's hand.

"Thanks. I'll bring him back as soon as I can," Phoebe said, slipping her arm through Daniel's. She pulled him safely away from the woman and then gave him a wink. "You looked like you could use some help."

"Uh . . . I . . ." Daniel stared at her, still looking kind of freaked out.

"Uh-oh." Phoebe's hand flew to her mouth. "Did I just mess up? Was that some incredibly generous patron of the arts?"

Daniel pulled his arm away and took a deep breath. "Do I know you?" he asked.

"No. I'm Phoebe Halliwell. I just wanted to say . . . um, great party," Phoebe replied lamely. This wasn't going the way she'd planned. She'd figured Daniel would flirt with her and she'd flirt back, which is what usually happened when you introduced yourself to a cute guy while you were wearing a killer outfit and having a good hair day. But Daniel was staring at her as if she were some kind of monster.

"I mean, I'm so happy I could come and represent my paper. I write a column for the *Bay Mirror*," she rushed on. "Maybe you've read it? 'Ask Phoebe'?"

He began to back away from her. "No."

"Oh, well, it's just an advice column. It's not about art or anything," Phoebe said. "But I'm really interested in your emerging artists project. . . ."

"Thanks. Bye." Daniel turned and pushed his way through the crowd without a backward glance.

Phoebe felt the blood rush to her cheeks.

What was going on? The guy had literally run away from her!

"Hey! How did it go?" Piper asked, rushing over to Phoebe. "Did you get his number?"

Phoebe whirled to face her sister. "Do I have food in my teeth?" She smiled widely.

"No." Piper frowned.

"Smeared lipstick? Runny mascara?" Phoebe grabbed Piper's glass of champagne and took a sip.

"Uh . . . no, none of the above," Piper replied. "Why?"

"Because Daniel Lemond just acted as if I were the most repulsive thing on Earth," Phoebe said miserably. "So much for my big romance."

Chapter 2

"He might as well have yelled 'cooties!' and run away," Phoebe complained on Monday morning. "I was so embarrassed."

On the other side of the kitchen table, Paige took a long gulp of her tea and sighed. "I know. You've been talking about it for two days now."

"Well, it was humiliating. Who knows how many people saw that?" Phoebe gasped as a new thought hit her. "What if one of the society page photographers caught it on film? I can see the headline now: 'Romantic Advisor Strikes Out.' Nobody will read my column anymore. I'll be ruined!"

"Somehow I doubt that one less-than-stellar conversation with a total stranger is going to end your career," Piper said from the stove. She was whipping up an omelet with one hand and feeding Wyatt in his high chair with the other.

"Besides, you give advice on more than just

romance," Paige pointed out. She sipped her tea and grimaced. "No one will care if you bombed with a guy."

Phoebe studied her half sister. "What's with that tea? You keep making faces every time you drink."

"It's not the tea, it's me," Paige said. "I woke up this morning with the worst sore throat. I was hoping hot tea would help, but it's not."

"Yikes. Sorry you feel bad, honey, but stay away from me," Phoebe told her. "I have to do an amazing column this week just in case you're both wrong about my future career doom. I can't afford to get sick."

"And stay away from Wyatt," Piper put in. "Leo's barely ever home these days, so I'm on full-time child-care duty. The last thing I need is Wyatt catching a cold."

"He already did," Paige said. "I cured it."

"Excuse me?" Piper asked.

"When you guys were at the museum party. Wyatt was sick, so I vanquished his cold with a potion."

"Nice work," Phoebe said. "But I guess you managed to catch it yourself first."

Paige frowned. "That doesn't make any sense. If I vanquished the cold, it should be gone. In both of us. I didn't make it a Wyatt-specific spell."

"Then maybe it didn't really work," Phoebe said.

"But Wyatt felt better right away. And he's

still fine." Paige coughed and took another sip of tea. "I don't get it."

"I don't, either. Sorry." Phoebe sighed and stood up. "I have to get to work." She shuffled toward the door, her expression glum.

"Cheer up!" Piper called after her. "Maybe you'll meet a cute guy in Starbucks this morning."

"Yeah, and when I try to flirt with him, he'll bolt," Phoebe called back. She had to face the truth. It had been months without romance, and now she was driving men away. There was only one explanation. She'd lost her mojo.

"Hey, Phoebes! How was your weekend?"

Phoebe peered over the top of her coffee cup. Her assistant, Ryan, was grinning at her from his desk outside her office. "Why? What did you hear?" she asked suspiciously. Had her Daniel Lemond humiliation really made it to the society page?

Ryan's smile faltered. "Huh?" he asked, confused.

"Never mind," Phoebe mumbled, heading into her office. "Do I have any messages?"

"Nope. But there's something waiting for you on your desk." Ryan hopped up and followed her to her door.

"Is it ticking?" Phoebe cracked. Then she got a good look at her desk—and at the sweet little vase full of daisies that sat on it. "Flowers? Who are they from?"

"There was no note," Ryan said. "But the billing address was the San Francisco Museum of Modern Art."

"Oh." She grabbed the vase and moved it to the windowsill behind her desk, where she wouldn't have to look at it and be reminded of the disastrous gala. "They probably sent them to everybody who went to the fund-raiser. They spent so much money on that party, it's amazing they have any left over to actually fund their art programs!"

Ryan shrugged. "They get people to donate things like the flowers. And the food and all that. Was it fun?"

"I guess so." Phoebe dropped into her chair and mustered up a smile for him. "They had one of the third world artists there, and that was really inspiring."

"Good." Ryan pulled out his PDA, where he kept track of Phoebe's schedule. "So you have a lunch with the managing editor today, and the staff meeting's at five."

"Okay. I want to get a lot of writing done this morning. Can you keep people from bothering me?" Phoebe asked. "There's a double-chocolate muffin in it for you."

"You got it." Ryan left, pulling her office door closed behind him. Phoebe settled down to work, pulling out the folder of letters from readers with low self-esteem. Maybe if she spent the morning telling other people how to feel better about themselves, she'd stop obsessing over her failure to flirt with Daniel Lemond.

But before she'd even gotten through a single letter, her office door opened and Ryan stuck his head in. "Visitor for you, Phoebe," he said.

She stared up at her assistant. "But I told you not to let anybody in."

"Oh." Ryan looked confused. "Yeah. Sorry. He asked to see you and I just . . . uh . . ."

"It's my fault," said Daniel Lemond, stepping into the room. "I wouldn't take no for an answer."

Phoebe's mouth fell open. Daniel wasn't wearing a tuxedo, but he looked just as good in jeans and a pullover. But what was he doing at her office?

"What are you doing here?" Phoebe blurted out.

Daniel raised his eyebrows. "I wanted to make sure you got my flowers."

"Oh. *Oh.*" Phoebe spun around and grabbed the vase of daisies. "I thought they were just a little gift from the museum."

"I knew I should've put a note on them," Daniel said. "Although this way I had an excuse to come see you."

Phoebe couldn't believe it. He was looking her right in the eye, smiling, and *flirting*. It was the exact opposite of his behavior the other night.

Ryan was still standing in the doorway, watching with a big goofy smile on his face. "Thanks, Ry," Phoebe said.

He nodded and kept on grinning.

"You can go now," she said. "Ryan?"

"Hmm?"

"Thanks. You can get back to work."

"Oh." Ryan's face fell. "Okay." He stepped out of her office and closed the door behind him.

Phoebe turned her attention back to Daniel. "Have a seat," she said, trying to cover her confusion. "How did you know where I worked?"

"You told me, remember?" Daniel dropped into her guest chair. "'Ask Phoebe.' It's my favorite column."

"It is?" Phoebe asked doubtfully.

"Absolutely. I never miss it. You're very insightful." Daniel leaned forward. "In fact, your advice to other people has helped me figure out a problem or two of my own."

"That's wonderful!" Phoebe beamed at him. "It's exactly what I want to hear. I always hope that I'm giving sort of universal advice, you know? That people can take what I say to one person and apply it to all sorts of things in their own experience."

"Then you succeed," Daniel told her. "You really know how to get to the root of your readers' problems and solve them in a no-nonsense way. And everybody can benefit from that sort of understanding. I know I do."

"But at the museum gala, I got the impression that you'd never even heard of me," Phoebe said.

"I have to apologize for that. I'm afraid I must have seemed rude," Daniel said. "I didn't mean to be; I was so preoccupied with making the event perfect that I wasn't able to talk to you for as long as I wanted to."

"You didn't seem to want to talk to me at all," Phoebe pointed out.

"I'm sorry you thought that, but nothing could be further from the truth, Phoebe," he said. "You were the most beautiful woman at the gala. You're the only one I wanted to talk to, honestly. But I was working. I had to keep on top of all the party details. I hope you can forgive me."

Daniel's dark blue eyes never left hers as he spoke, and Phoebe found herself hanging on his every word. After he'd blown her off so thoroughly the other day, it was almost impossible to believe that he was sitting in her office complimenting her column. And complimenting *her.* "I guess I can forgive you," she said. "I know I get overly absorbed in work sometimes too."

"Great." Daniel sighed in relief. "I'd hate to think you were angry with me. I was worrying about it all weekend."

"Really? I was worried that I'd done something wrong to make you not like me," Phoebe admitted.

"That would be impossible," Daniel assured her. "You're perfect. I'm the one to blame. But I'm hoping we can get past our rough start and be good friends. Well, actually, I'm hoping we can be more than that."

Phoebe opened her mouth, then closed it again. This was feeling more and more like a

dream. Daniel certainly believed in getting right
to the point!

"Will you let me make it up to you over
dinner?" he went on. "Tomorrow night?"

"Sure." She smiled. "Dinner sounds like fun."

"It will be," he said. "It will be perfect. I
promise."

"And then what happened?" Daniel asked,
reaching over to refill Phoebe's wineglass.

"I moved back here, to San Francisco," she
told him. "It wasn't the same without Grams,
but I just knew I had to be with my sisters."

"Even though you all fought a lot?"

"Absolutely. My sisters are the most important thing in the world to me." Phoebe fell silent
for a moment, thinking of Prue, her oldest sister,
who had died fighting a demon a few years ago.
"We all got to know each other really well—and
love each other even more than we did before,"
she added quietly. "Thank God I came back to
live with them."

"Well, I'm certainly glad you did," Daniel
said. "Otherwise I never would have met you."

She looked up at him, his face glowing in the
dim light of the candlelit restaurant. He'd been
listening to her tell her entire life story all
through dinner, and he seemed enthralled.
She'd never met a guy who was so interested in
all the little details of her past. "So you're happy
you met me even though I've been boring you

with stories of my life all night?" she asked.

"Nothing you say is boring, Phoebe," he told her.

"I don't know. Three hours of listening to me talk about me seems pretty dull," she joked. "I can't believe I hogged the conversation this whole time. Tell me about you."

"Now *that* would be boring," he said. "Besides, we're done eating. Talking about me will have to wait until next time."

"Are you sure? We can always order another dessert," Phoebe said. "I'd never say no to a second helping of chocolate mousse."

Daniel laughed and signaled the waiter for the check. "Seriously, my life is too tedious to discuss. It makes me sad just thinking about its tediousness."

"It can't be that bad. You've got an exciting job, at least," Phoebe said. "I always thought I'd make a great event planner, but then I threw a surprise party for Piper one time and it was a total disaster. But you're obviously the maestro of party planning."

"What happened?" Daniel asked as he signed the bill. "At Piper's party?"

"Oh. She wasn't surprised, for one thing. I kinda forgot that part of it—I didn't have anybody set up to distract her. So she walked in while we were blowing up balloons."

"Oops." Daniel chuckled as they headed out to his car. "That is rule number one of surprise parties."

"But that wasn't even the worst thing. I also forgot to confirm with the caterers, so they never made the fabulous gourmet birthday cake I wanted, and I ended up having to get her a cake from the grocery store. The only one they had left was shaped like a motorcycle and decorated in bright blue icing."

"I take it that's not Piper's style?" Daniel asked.

Phoebe snorted. "Hardly. Plus, she could barely choke it down. She's a chef, so she's got a *very* refined palate."

"Really? A chef?" Daniel asked, pulling out of the parking lot. "Does she have her own restaurant?"

"Oh, no." Phoebe narrowed her eyes at him. "You're not getting me to talk about my sister. I don't even know how I ended up telling you the surprise party story. I was trying to ask about *your* job, and suddenly here I am babbling about myself again."

"But I want to hear about you. You're fascinating to me," Daniel insisted.

"I'm describing a birthday cake from a million years ago. Trust me, that is not fascinating," Phoebe said. "I wouldn't even go as far as mildly interesting."

"That's because you aren't sitting in my place," Daniel said. "Having an honest, open conversation with a smart, beautiful, funny woman is a rare occurrence."

Phoebe glanced at him. "Those sound like the

words of a man who's been hurt before," she said.

He blushed a little, then shrugged. "Who hasn't? Didn't you tell me you're still recovering from a divorce?"

"Yeah," Phoebe said. But she didn't want to think about Cole, her half-demon, half-human ex. "In fact, it's kind of surprising that I am talking to you so honestly and openly, considering how much I got burned," she added.

"I hope that's a sign that you feel comfortable with me," Daniel said. "Because I'd like to take you out again, Phoebe."

Phoebe felt a little rush of pleasure. She'd had such a good time with Daniel tonight that she didn't want the date to end. And it seemed he felt the same way. "I'd like that too. As long as I get to hear *your* life story next time, like you promised."

"We'll see," he said. "First you have to finish yours. You only got up to the part where you moved back to San Francisco. I have a feeling all the really juicy stuff has happened since then."

"You're right about that," she murmured. Of course, she couldn't exactly tell him how she and her sisters had realized they were witches—and not just any witches, but the Charmed Ones. And she couldn't tell him about the tons of demons and warlocks and other evil things they'd fought and defeated in the years since she'd come back to Halliwell Manor. In fact, there wasn't a whole lot she could tell him about her real life. So much for the honest, open conversation! "Still, I'd rather hear about your childhood and your family and stuff. It's only fair—you know all about mine. We can take turns," she said.

Daniel didn't answer. He pulled up in front of the Manor and stopped the car.

Phoebe glanced up at the house. She loved it, and she loved being there with her sisters. But right now, all she wanted to do was stay in the car with Daniel. The idea of leaving him seemed completely depressing. "Or you could come inside with me," she blurted out. "And tell me your story tonight."

Daniel stared at her as if she'd lost her mind. "Come in?" he repeated.

"Yeah. My nephew will be asleep already, and nobody will bother us," she said.

"Uh, I don't think so." Daniel unhooked his seat belt, leaped out of the car, and practically ran around to open Phoebe's door. The expression on his face was the same one he'd had when she tried to talk to him at the museum party— the expression that said he couldn't wait to get away from her.

"O-kay." She climbed out of the car and looked up at him. "Well . . . good night." She stood on her tiptoes to give him a kiss, but he backed away and didn't meet her eye.

"Yeah. Good night." Daniel slammed the car door, jogged back around to his own side, and peeled away without another word.

Stunned, Phoebe watched him go. What had happened to the great guy she'd had dinner with? She turned and walked up to the house.

"How was the date?" Paige asked as soon as Phoebe walked into the living room. She was lying on the couch bundled in an afghan and sipping tea.

"Ninety percent perfect and ten percent awful," Phoebe replied. She threw herself down onto the overstuffed chair and grabbed a throw pillow to hug. "I don't get it."

"Get what?" Piper asked, coming down the stairs.

"Daniel. We had this amazing dinner and he seemed really into me—he even asked me out again. And then when we got here, he just took off. It was exactly like that night at the party."

Piper perched on the arm of the couch. "Men suck."

Phoebe glanced up at her. "Oh, really?"

"I've seen Leo for about ten minutes since our anniversary," Piper complained. "He didn't even give me a card."

"Wow. I think that calls for some serious yelling at," Paige said.

"He's not around long enough to yell at," Piper replied. "He's always off taking care of this new charge of his, that Kerria girl."

"Why? Does she have some kind of extreme evil stalker?" Phoebe asked.

"Who knows?" Piper rolled her eyes. "Anyway,

we're talking about Daniel. Maybe he's just too weird, Phoebes."

"But I like him," Phoebe moaned. "I feel totally comfortable with him. I even told him about that time Grams caught me cutting my hair to look more like Captain Kangaroo."

"What? You've never even told *me* about that!" Paige cried. She started to laugh, but it turned into a cough.

"Maybe that's what drove him away," Piper joked. "I'm not sure guys want to hear about the Captain Kangaroo phase of a girl's life."

Phoebe sat bolt upright, replaying the night's conversation in her mind. "Oh my God, you're right," she said. "I spent the entire date talking about myself. I must have come off as the biggest egomaniac ever. No wonder he ran."

"I thought you said he asked you out again," Paige said.

"Well, yeah . . ."

"Was that before or after you did the Phoebe Halliwell Biography special?" Piper asked.

"After. On the way home," Phoebe replied. "Now I'm confused again. If it wasn't because I was so self-involved, then why was he so weird when we got here?"

"What exactly happened?" Paige asked.

"We got to the Manor, I invited him in, and he went bizarro on me," Phoebe said. She looked from Piper to Paige. "You don't think I scared him off by asking him in, do you?"

"Guys usually want to get invited in," Piper said slowly. "Don't they?"

"Maybe he's shy, though." Paige blew her nose loudly. "If he is, he could have gotten scared."

"Oh, no. I was moving too fast for him." Phoebe sighed, depressed. "It's not fair. I finally meet a guy I really like and I'm too pushy to keep him around. Why didn't I just chill?"

"But it's not as if you'll never see him again. You have another date," Piper said.

"We didn't make any definite plan," Phoebe replied. "You know what that means—the next date will never really happen."

"Then *you* make the definite plan," Paige told her. "Call him up and say, 'We're going out on Friday night.'"

"Won't that seem even more pushy and bossy?" Phoebe asked.

"Maybe. But what have you got to lose?" Piper said. "In fact, I'm going to take that advice myself. Next time I see my husband, I'll just tell him we're rescheduling our anniversary date for tomorrow night. And I won't take no for an answer."

"Good for you," Paige mumbled. "Now both of you go away so I can be miserable in peace."

"Why don't you just go up to bed?" Phoebe asked.

Paige gazed at the stairs with bleary eyes. "It's too far away," she said. "My head is so stuffed up that I get dizzy just from standing."

Phoebe shot Piper a look, and Piper nodded. "Okay, Operation Sister Support is underway. I'll help you upstairs and Phoebe will get more tea and some water."

"And another box of tissues," Paige called wearily as Phoebe headed for the kitchen.

Phoebe smiled to herself. Maybe bossiness ran in the family!

"Leo! Breakfast!" Piper called the next morning. Her husband hadn't gotten home until almost two in the morning the night before, so she hadn't woken him up yet. But now Wyatt was dressed and finishing up his bottle, Phoebe had already left for work, and it was time for Leo to get up.

"Did you give him your anniversary date ultimatum yet?" Paige asked from the other side of the table. Her face was buried in her arms, so Piper could barely hear her. Paige's place mat was littered with tissues and she didn't lift her head even to talk.

"Not yet. I will this morning," Piper said. "Are you taking anything for that cold?"

"I tried, but I can't. Decongestants make me puke."

"That's just the kind of talk a man wants to hear first thing in the morning," Leo cracked, coming into the kitchen. He dropped a kiss on Wyatt's head and one on Piper's.

"Sorry," Paige mumbled.

"I made pancakes," Piper told Leo. "Strawberry. Your favorite."

Leo winced. "Thanks, honey, but I really don't have time. I'm just gonna grab a banana and go."

Piper narrowed her eyes at him. "Go where?"

"I've got to check in on my new charge. She's in way over her head," Leo said.

Piper felt a rush of annoyance. She knew Leo's Whitelighter duties were important, but so was their marriage. "Leo, has it even occurred to you that we skipped our anniversary this year?" she asked.

"Of course," he said. "I told you I was sorry."

"That's not good enough. I want to reschedule," Piper said. "In fact, I have rescheduled. We're doing it tonight—the whole thing. Going out to a candlelight dinner, getting all romantic . . ." She stood up and slipped her arms around him.

Leo grinned and reached down to brush his lips against hers. "Sounds perfect," he murmured.

Paige sneezed.

They both turned to look at her.

"My bad," she said. "Didn't mean to spoil the moment."

"Wait a minute," Leo said. "How can we go out tonight? Our babysitter is sick."

Piper took in Paige's rumpled pajamas, bed head, and red nose. Leo was right. They couldn't leave Wyatt with her in this condition. She groaned. "We're never going to get our dinner, are we?"

"Yes, you are!" Paige stood up quickly, then grabbed on to the chair back to keep from toppling over. "You've just given me the perfect excuse!"

"For what?" Leo asked.

"For curing my cold. I got rid of Wyatt's cold using magic, but I couldn't use that spell on me because it would be for personal gain, right?"

"Right . . . ," Piper said slowly.

"But if I do it for you guys, so you can go out and get all lovey-dovey, then it's not for personal gain." Paige pulled an envelope down from the cabinet, poured the herbs inside it into a potion bottle, and added some boiling water from the teapot. "It's a good thing I saved the leftover potion," she said happily.

"Using magic to make yourself feel better still seems suspiciously like personal gain to me," Leo said.

"But if it helps us get our one night alone together, I'm all for it," Piper added.

"Okay." Paige shook up the bottle, threw it to the ground at her feet, and quickly said the spell: "Sickness like an evil, loosen your bond. Vanquished are you. Be gone!"

Piper watched closely, astonished at the instant change in her sister. Paige's bloodshot eyes cleared up, her swollen nose returned to normal, and she took a deep breath.

"Now *that's* what I'm talking about," Paige said, smiling.

"Feel better?" Piper asked.

"Good enough to babysit for however long you two need me," Paige replied. "So feel free to make it a long night."

"Great." Piper turned to her husband. "So now there's nothing standing in the way of us and romance. Right?"

Leo made a face. "I know I've been working too much lately, sweetie. I'm sorry. I promise I'll be home in time tonight. We'll have the most perfect late anniversary ever."

Phoebe, sitting behind her desk, stared at her phone. She'd already picked it up twice to call Daniel, but she'd chickened out both times. What was she supposed to say? *Hi, Daniel, sorry I had the nerve to invite you in on the first date?*

"You're being a freak," Ryan commented from the doorway of her office. "You had one date. You barely even know him. What's the big deal?"

"He thinks I'm easy," Phoebe said. "He thought I was inviting him into my house to . . . you know . . ."

"How do you know what he thinks unless you call him?" Ryan asked. "Maybe he suddenly remembered he left the oven on or something and that's why he took off."

"You really think so?"

Ryan squirmed uncomfortably. "No. But still, I don't see why you care so much."

"I'm not sure why," she admitted. "There's just something about him that makes me really like him. He's . . . magnetic."

"Then call him." Ryan shook his head.

The phone rang, making them both jump. Phoebe snatched it up. "Phoebe Halliwell."

"Phoebe, hi. It's Daniel," said a deep, luscious voice on the other side.

Her mouth dropped open in surprise—and panic. "It's him," she mouthed to Ryan.

"Phoebe?" Daniel said.

"Yes! I'm here!" She forced herself to take a deep breath. "Um, hi. I'm glad you called."

"I realize things ended a little weirdly the other night," Daniel began.

"I'm so embarrassed," Phoebe cut in. "We were having such a wonderful time that I just hated the idea of saying good night. I thought you could come in and we'd keep talking, but I guess maybe I gave you the wrong idea. I didn't mean to push you or anything—"

"Stop babbling!" Ryan whispered.

Phoebe's mouth snapped shut. What was her problem? Every time she talked to Daniel, she turned into a fourteen-year-old girl with a crush.

"Well, you were moving a little fast for me," Daniel said.

Phoebe smiled. "Yeah, I know. Sorry."

"It's okay. You know I really like you, Phoebe. Are we still on for another date?" he asked.

"Absolutely."

"How about tonight? I know it's short notice . . ."

"No, tonight is perfect," Phoebe said quickly. "I'd love to."

"I was thinking I'd cook. Do you want to come to my place around eight?"

"Sure. Yes. What should I bring?"

"Just your beautiful self," Daniel said. "I'll see you then."

"Wait!" Phoebe cried, not wanting him to hang up. "Um . . . what are you making?"

"I have a great recipe for a sausage gumbo," Daniel said. "Why? Are you a vegetarian?"

"No," Phoebe said.

"Is there some food you hate that I should know about?"

"No," she replied.

"Oh." Daniel didn't say anything for a moment, and Phoebe cringed. She'd made this whole conversation really awkward. But she still didn't want him to hang up. "Okay, well, see you tonight, Phoebe," he finally said.

"Eight o'clock?"

"Yes."

"And you're sure I can't bring anything?"

"Yes. I really have to get back to work now," Daniel said gently.

"Okay. Bye." Phoebe hung up the phone and looked at Ryan.

"What was that all about?" he asked.

"I kinda didn't want to get off the phone," she said. "I sounded stupid, right?"

"A little. But what did he say about the other night?" Ryan asked.

"He said I was moving too fast."

Ryan's eyebrows shot up. "Ouch."

"Is that bad?" Phoebe thought about it. "Oh my God, that *is* bad! Why didn't I realize that? It sounded totally fine when he said it. Almost like a compliment."

"Trust me, it's not a compliment. He sounds like a jerk to me."

"Well, he's not," Phoebe snapped.

"Calm down. It's not like I insulted *you*," Ryan said.

Phoebe took a deep breath. He was right. Why did she feel so protective of Daniel, anyway?

"All I mean is that he said you were moving too fast, and then he invited you to his place for tonight," Ryan pointed out. "How does that make sense? He's moving pretty fast too."

"I know." Phoebe couldn't help it. A big smile crept across her face.

Ryan shook his head and turned to leave. "You obviously like this guy way too much."

Phoebe sat back in her chair and thought about her date with Daniel. She couldn't wait!

Chapter 3

"Wow, look at you!" Paige cried that night, taking in Piper's body-hugging red dress. "Is that Phoebe's?"

"Of course," Piper said with a grin. "I go out so rarely that I don't have any sexy outfits. I already wore my one hot dress to the museum gala last weekend."

"Phoebe's closet always comes through," Paige said. She peeked into the living room to check on Wyatt, asleep in his bouncy seat. "So where are you guys having dinner?"

"At Le Colonial," Piper said. "And then we're going dancing. I can't wait. I feel like I haven't had a single conversation with Leo in months— at least not a conversation about anything other than Wyatt or Leo's charges."

"You two need to reconnect," Paige agreed. "Parenting is stressful enough without supernatural demands on your time."

Right on cue, white light filled the foyer, and Leo orbed in.

"There's my Prince Charming," Piper said, going over to kiss him hello.

"Stay away from me!" he cried, throwing his hands up to block her. He ran into the kitchen.

"That's not how it usually goes in fairy tales," Paige commented.

Piper's mouth set in a grim line and she followed him. Paige hesitated, then went after her.

"What is going on?" Piper demanded. Leo was drinking orange juice straight from the carton.

"Ew," Paige said. "I hope you'll be finishing that, because—"

Leo slammed the empty carton down onto the counter.

"Never mind," Paige finished.

"I've been coughing for three hours and now I'm starting to get a sinus headache," Leo said. "I don't want to get sick. Not tonight."

Frowning, Piper went over and peered into his face. "Your eyes are all glassy."

"Yeah."

"And you're all sweaty."

"I know."

"You've got a cold," Piper said. "A bad one."

Leo turned away. "I don't want to get you sick. But don't worry, I'll just run upstairs and take some aspirin and then we can go to dinner." He took two steps, then doubled over coughing.

Paige winced.

"You sound terrible," Piper told Leo. "Does it hurt?"

"Kind of," he admitted. "My throat is killing me, even when I don't cough. But it doesn't matter. It's our anniversary, sort of. I'm not going to let a little cold get in the way of that." He coughed again.

"As attractive as the coughing fits are, I think I'm going to have to take a rain check on tonight," Piper said slowly. "You're way too sick to go out."

"No, I'm not."

"Leo, your breathing sounds like Darth Vader," Piper said. "You're completely sick."

Leo slumped down into one of the kitchen chairs. "You're right. I'm so sorry, honey."

"You shouldn't be sorry," Piper replied. "Paige should."

"Me?" Paige squeaked. "Why?"

"Because you gave him this cold," Piper cried. "And I don't mean you breathed on him when you were sick. I mean you gave him this cold with your spell."

"I did not," Paige said. "The spell only got rid of *my* cold. I didn't tell it to go anywhere else."

"This is the second time it's happened, though," Piper said. "The first time the cold disappeared from Wyatt and appeared in you. And now your cold vanished and reappeared in Leo."

"But the spell can't make that happen all by

itself," Paige protested. "I must've just given Leo my cold before I did the spell."

"I don't know," Leo put in. "It's pretty instantaneous. You said Wyatt got better immediately, and so did you this morning. But you got sick immediately and now I have too. I mean, I usually at least get the sniffles for a day or so before I start feeling this bad."

"I guess my cold did go from zero to sixty pretty fast too," Paige said.

"Face it. Your spell has side effects," Piper told her. "It's backfiring."

"Well . . . maybe I can tweak it," Paige suggested. "I'll reword it. And I'll add some fenugreek to the potion for Leo's sore throat." She rushed over to the herb cabinet and began gathering ingredients while she thought through the words of the spell. "Don't you worry, I'll cure you. I'm not going to let your anniversary dinner be ruined because of me."

"No, Paige," Leo said. "You've already done this spell once for personal gain. I can't let you do it again."

"It's not for personal gain," she argued. "It's for you two, not for me."

"Exactly. It's for *our* personal gain," Leo said. "You can't do that."

Piper looked skeptical. "Are you sure? Because she can get rid of the cold pretty fast. We'd still make our reservation at the restaurant."

"I'm sure. If Paige did the spell for me, she

might be obeying the letter of the personal gain law, but she wouldn't be obeying the spirit of it." Leo coughed again, and winced in pain. "I have to go lie down."

"Okay. I'll bring you up some tea in a few minutes," Piper called after him as he trudged toward the stairs.

"We *always* obey the letter of the law and not the spirit," Paige whispered to Piper.

"Well, maybe that's why the spell isn't working right," Piper said. She looked down at her red dress and sighed. "I don't think I'm ever going to get an anniversary dinner."

"I can't believe you made this ice cream," Phoebe said. "Who *makes* ice cream?"

Daniel paused with his spoon halfway to his mouth, a brief expression of panic flickering across his face. "You don't like it?"

"Are you kidding? It's delicious," Phoebe assured him. "I'm just in shock that there's a man in existence who can work all day and then come home and whip up a gourmet meal. And make ice cream for dessert. I probably would have gone for the Häagen-Dazs, sadly."

"Then it's a good thing I was cooking, not you," he joked. "Really, it's no big deal. I have one of those ice-cream maker machines. I just thought you'd like it."

"I do. It's great. You're great." Phoebe narrowed her eyes at him. "In fact, you're too good to be true. What's your secret?"

Daniel pushed back his chair and stood up, almost knocking over the vase of peonies on the table. "Uh, I'm a closet klutz," he said. "My secret is out."

Phoebe laughed. "There must be something worse than that."

"Nope. How about you? What's your secret?" he asked, taking her empty bowl and heading for the kitchen.

"I don't think I have any secrets left." Phoebe followed him, bringing their wineglasses to the sink. "Between tonight and the last time, I think I've told you every single thing there is to know about me." *Except for the fact that I'm a witch,* she added silently.

"I don't know what your favorite movie is," he said.

"Neither do I," Phoebe replied. "Every time I see a movie I love, I think that one is my favorite. And then I see a different one that I love, and I change my mind." She put the glasses down and turned to face him. "I'm not that way about guys, though. Don't worry."

"Good." Daniel slipped his arms around her waist. "Because I don't want you to change your mind about me."

"I won't," she whispered. "I think you're perfect and nothing could change that." She stood on tiptoe and kissed him, smiling as he tightened his arms and kissed her back. It had been a long time since she'd been into a guy as much as she was into Daniel.

She pulled away abruptly. "Wait a minute. You're doing it again," she said.

"Doing what?"

"Getting me to talk about myself instead of you." Phoebe took his hand and led him back out to the combo living and dining room of his apartment. "So talk. What's *your* favorite movie?"

"Do you really want to discuss movies right now?" Daniel asked, his voice low and sexy. He moved toward her for another kiss, and Phoebe forgot all about wanting to talk.

But after a few minutes, Daniel pulled away. "It's getting late," he murmured.

"And I have to be at work at the crack of dawn tomorrow," Phoebe said with a sigh. "Early meeting."

"I guess we'd better say good night, then." Daniel ran his hand through his hair. "I have a morning meeting too."

"I don't even know where you work," Phoebe told him as she gathered up her purse and her jacket. "Is your office anywhere near mine? We could grab lunch tomorrow, if you want."

"Uh, no. My office is over in Oakland, believe it or not." He pulled open the door. "I'll walk you to your car."

"Okay." Phoebe practically skipped down the short stairway that led to the front door of Daniel's building. Just being around him made her feel special. He was such a gentleman! "Thank you for dinner. It was incredible."

"I'm glad you liked it."

At her car, she turned for another kiss. But just as her lips brushed Daniel's, a screech cut through the night. Phoebe jumped, then dropped immediately into a fighting stance. She'd taken martial arts classes and perfected her skills so she'd always be ready to battle a demon on a moment's notice.

Another screech rang through the air, followed by a crashing sound.

"What is that?" Daniel asked, glancing around nervously. He shot Phoebe a worried look. "Are you okay?"

She suddenly realized how bizarre she must appear—all dressed up and standing in a karate stance in the middle of the sidewalk. Quickly, she straightened up. "Yeah. I was just startled."

"I think it's a cat," Daniel told her.

"A cat. Right." Phoebe felt her face heat up with embarrassment. Not a demon, a cat. "That's one loud kitty."

More screeches and more crashes came from the alley next to Daniel's building. He led the way over. Phoebe followed him, her heart still pounding. She usually didn't get so freaked out, even by demons. But she'd been so wrapped up in Daniel that she'd almost forgotten the world outside.

"Two cats," Daniel said. "Look."

Phoebe peered over his shoulder. Halfway

down the alley, a tabby cat stood on top of a pile of old shingles. A large calico crouched in the darkness nearby, hissing and growling. Suddenly, the tabby pounced. The two cats became nothing but a blur of flashing claws and teeth, both of them yowling the entire time.

"They're going to kill each other!" Phoebe cried. "We have to stop them."

"How can you stop alley cats from fighting?" Daniel asked. "I guess I could try throwing something at them. You know, to scare them off."

But the cats had already stopped. Both stood staring at Daniel and Phoebe, their green eyes luminous in the darkness.

"Why are they looking at us that way?" Daniel asked.

The tabby mewed and padded over to them. It rubbed against Daniel's leg.

"I think you have an admirer," Phoebe said.

"But why did they just stop? They were really going at it," Daniel said.

The calico ran over and threw itself down at Daniel's feet, rolling over to show its stomach. Grinning, he bent down and rubbed its tummy. Phoebe laughed.

"I guess they were only playing," Daniel said.

"I don't know about that. They sounded seriously angry." Phoebe couldn't believe the change in the two cats—they were acting as if Daniel were a huge stalk of catnip. "You obviously have a way with animals."

"Not really. I barely remember to feed my fish." Daniel stood up. "Well, let's get you into your car before they start fighting again."

Phoebe took his hand as they walked back over to the car. "Thanks again," she told him. "See you soon?"

"Count on it."

Dear Phoebe,
Help! I met the greatest girl, but her insecurity is driving me insane. She won't let me see her without makeup on, or with her hair a mess, or when she's feeling bloated—she's got an entire list! How can I make her understand that I think she's beautiful no matter what she looks like?
Frustrated

Dear Frustrated,
Sounds like your insecure girl has some control issues, as well. She wants to control how you see her—always looking her absolute best—because she thinks it will help her control how you feel about her. Lucky for her, you're already smitten. My advice? Show her the letter you wrote me. That should tell her all she needs to know!

Phoebe glanced up from her computer on Thursday afternoon. The light on her phone was on, but she hadn't heard it ring for at least ten minutes. And now that she thought about it, she'd never found out who was calling ten minutes ago. Usually Ryan gave Phoebe her messages right away. She looked out the office door to his desk. He was sitting back in his chair, feet up on the desk and gabbing away with a big smile on his face. Phoebe sighed. She liked the guy, but he had a habit of letting his personal life get in the way of work sometimes.

"Ryan!" she called.

He jumped, yanked his feet off the desk, and hit the Hold button. "Sorry, Phoebes," he said. "It's Daniel."

"Huh?" Phoebe said.

"Daniel. Lemond? The guy you're dating?"

"Wait," Phoebe replied, confused. "You've been talking to Daniel for ten minutes?"

"I guess." Ryan shrugged. "He's really cool, you know. Better than most of your boyfriends."

Phoebe frowned. "But the other day you said he was a jerk."

"No way. I was wrong," Ryan said. "He's a keeper."

"Okay." Phoebe felt a wave of uneasiness pass through her. Ryan wasn't usually so fickle. She picked up her phone and hit the button. "Hello?"

"Hi, sweetie," Daniel said.

Phoebe's pulse sped up. He'd called her sweetie! "Hi yourself," she said.

"I was just calling to say I miss you."

"Even though you saw me last night?" she asked.

"Absolutely," Daniel said softly. "I can't wait to see you again."

"Me either," Phoebe told him.

"I'd love to talk, but I have to get back to work," Daniel said. "Your assistant kept me on the phone for so long."

"I know. Sorry." Phoebe glanced out at Ryan. "I'm not sure what that was all about."

"No problem. As long as I got to hear your voice, I'm happy," Daniel said. "Talk to you soon."

Phoebe fought her urge to keep talking so he wouldn't hang up. "Okay. Bye."

She hung up the phone and sat back, enjoying the warm feeling that Daniel always left her with. "What did he say?" Ryan asked, sticking his head into her office.

"That he misses me." Phoebe happily swung her chair from side to side, but Ryan made a face.

"He misses you? That's kind of cheesy," he commented.

"It is not. It's sweet." Though now that he brought it up, that did seem kind of like an eighth-grade thing to say. "It sounded sweet when he said it, anyway," she added.

"When are you gonna see him again?"

"I'm not sure," Phoebe said. "I wish I could see him tonight. It's like I'm addicted or something. But we didn't make any plans."

"So what? You guys are into each other. Just go over and see him." Ryan tossed a folder onto her desk. "Today's interesting letters. I'm gonna go get some coffee. You want any?"

"Sure. Thanks." Phoebe bit her lip, thinking about his suggestion. Maybe she should go see Daniel tonight. She could drop by after work, maybe bring him flowers or something. After all, he'd been nice enough to cook for her. It would be polite to make some kind of gesture in return.

As soon as she finished up her last phone call of the day, Phoebe grabbed her bag and headed out to the little flower shop on the corner near the paper's office. She bought a huge bouquet of calla lilies and drove over to Daniel's apartment.

Heading up the stairs, Phoebe felt a moment of doubt. She'd been on two dates with this guy, and here she was delivering flowers to his door. It seemed kind of crazy. But every time she was with him, she liked him so much. It was just a little hard to remember why when he wasn't right there in front of her. Still, she'd come all the way here. She might as well go through with it.

Taking a deep breath, she knocked on the door.

A moment later, Daniel opened it. His face paled when he saw her. "Phoebe," he said.

Immediately she felt better. What had she been worried about? Of course she liked Daniel. He was amazing. "Hi. These are for you," she said, holding out the calla lilies.

Daniel just stood there gaping at her.

"I know it's usually the guy who's supposed to bring flowers, but I figured . . . well, I wanted to thank you for dinner last night." Phoebe took a step closer to him. "And I wanted to see you."

Daniel didn't move out of the doorway.

"Daniel? Can I come in?" she asked, her nervousness returning.

"No," he said, blocking her way.

Phoebe's eyebrows shot up. "Why not?"

"You should have told me you were coming," Daniel said in an agitated voice. "You can't just show up like this. It won't work!"

As Phoebe watched, stunned, he stepped inside and closed the door—right in her face.

Chapter 4

"Okay, it's time to pull the plug on this thing," Piper announced on Friday morning. She stalked into the kitchen with Wyatt on her hip.

"That's what I was just telling her," Paige said, waving her fork at Phoebe. "Daniel is clearly a control freak. He's too weird. She has to dump him."

Phoebe sighed and took a sip of her coffee. "I hate when you guys gang up on me."

Piper settled Wyatt in his high chair and began feeding him his breakfast. "Actually, I was talking about Leo's cold. He's still completely sick, and I'm sick of it! I want you to do your cold-vanquishing spell on him, Paige."

"But he said not to," Paige reminded her.

"I know. But I can't take any more. The only time I've spent with my husband in the last month has been filled with him lying in bed and moaning while I bring him tea and tissues."

"You do look pretty harried," Phoebe put in. Piper hadn't even combed her hair yet this morning, and Piper *always* combed her hair.

"I've been taking care of Wyatt all by myself for ages." Piper sighed. "Between Leo's White-lighter duties and now this cold, he's no help at all. I'm starting to really resent him."

Phoebe turned to Paige. "Do the spell. Piper and Leo need some quality time together, and they still need that anniversary date."

"If you cure him this morning, we can go out tonight," Piper said. "Please?"

"All right. But I'm not taking the blame if Leo gets mad." Paige stood up to get the potion together.

"For the record, I do agree with Paige," Piper told Phoebe. "Daniel's weird. This is the third time he's been totally rude to you. He's cute, but no guy is cute enough to get away with slam-ming a door on you."

"He didn't *slam* it," Phoebe protested lamely.

"Phoebes," Piper began in her lecturing voice.

But right then, Phoebe's cell phone vibrated in the pocket of her blazer. Saved by the bell! "Sorry, gotta take this," she said, jumping up from the table. She hit the talk button on the phone. "Hello?"

"Phoebe? It's Daniel."

Phoebe caught her breath. She wanted to be mad at him, but just hearing his deep voice sent a chill up her spine. "Hi," she said, turning away from her sisters just as Paige began her spell to vanquish Leo's cold.

"I wanted to apologize for last night. I realize I was very rude," Daniel said regretfully. "I hope you can forgive me."

Something inside Phoebe longed to say *Of course*. But she forced herself to remember how upset she'd been, walking away from Daniel's apartment with a big stupid bunch of lilies. "You slammed the door in my face," she told him.

"I didn't *slam* it," he said.

She couldn't help herself. She smiled.

"But I shouldn't have done what I did," he added quickly. "I have no excuse."

Phoebe didn't know what to say. The truth was, just hearing him apologize was enough to make her forgive him. Still, she knew her sisters wouldn't be satisfied with that explanation. And maybe they were right. "How can you have no excuse?" she asked. "Why didn't you let me in?"

"I . . . I didn't want you to see my apartment. It was a mess," Daniel said.

"But I was there the night before and it was spotless," Phoebe reminded him.

"I know. I'm a slob. I just couldn't stand the idea of you seeing how much havoc I can wreak in a single day. You're so perfect and I want to be good enough for you."

Phoebe relaxed. It was impossible to stay mad at him when he said things like that. "Okay, you're forgiven. But I'm far from perfect. And you don't have to keep trying to impress me. You already have."

"Can I make it up to you tonight?" Daniel asked.

"I have a dinner," Phoebe said regretfully. "My boss throws these working dinners once a month and the whole writing staff has to go."

"How about dessert, then?" he asked. "You can come over after your dinner. I'll have everything ready. My way of saying sorry for yesterday."

"You already said you were sorry. You don't have to do anything else."

"But I want to say it in person," he murmured.

Phoebe's pulse sped up. "Well, if you put it that way . . ."

"See you tonight, then," Daniel said.

She hung up the phone just as Leo came bounding into the kitchen. "Morning, everyone!" he practically sang.

"Feeling better?" Piper asked.

"Much." Leo grabbed a piece of toast off Piper's plate and took a big bite. "What a relief. I could barely even breathe, I was so congested."

"Sounds like you're finally fit for that anniversary date," Piper said. "Let's do it tonight."

Leo's face fell. "I don't know, honey. I have a lot of catching up to do. I haven't been able to check on any of my charges for two days, and Kerria just called for me this morning. I have to make sure she's okay. She's not in complete control of her powers yet."

"Then you better get going," Piper said. "Because I *know* you're going to be home by seven thirty so we can go out to dinner."

Her tone of voice was enough for Leo. He simply nodded. "I'll see you then." He kissed her, gave Paige and Phoebe a wave, and orbed out of the room.

"He obviously doesn't even care about our anniversary," Piper complained. "I have to nag him into going on a date with me."

"He's just busy," Phoebe assured her. "And men are clueless."

"Speaking of clueless, that was Daniel, wasn't it?" Paige asked.

"Yeah. I'm going to see him tonight," Phoebe said happily.

"To break up with him?" Piper asked.

"No. He explained the whole thing. He didn't want me to see his messy apartment. He's trying to impress me and he figured I'd be turned off if I thought he was a slob."

Phoebe's sisters both stared at her as if she were an idiot.

"What?" Phoebe asked.

"That makes no sense," Piper replied. "How bad could the mess have been? And why couldn't he just step out into the hall if he didn't want you to come in?"

Phoebe frowned. "I don't know."

"Seriously," Paige agreed. "He didn't have to slam the door on you. He could have said 'My place is a mess, but thank you for the flowers.'"

"That's true." Phoebe went back over the conversation with Daniel in her mind. "I don't know, it all made sense when Daniel said it."

"So are you going to dump him or not?" Paige asked.

Phoebe thought about it. Every time she saw Daniel or talked to him on the phone, he left her feeling almost drunk with happiness. Wasn't that remarkable enough to earn him another chance? "I don't think so," she said slowly. "He seemed truly sorry about yesterday. I think I'll give him one more shot."

Piper and Paige didn't say anything else. But Phoebe could tell they thought she was crazy.

And she was beginning to wonder if they were right.

"Are you sure I can come in this time?" Phoebe asked as soon as Daniel opened the door that night.

He smiled his adorable crooked smile. "I scrubbed the whole place just for you."

Phoebe stepped inside, stopping to give him a quick kiss. "You didn't need to do that. If you're a slob, you're a slob. I don't care. I want to know the real you."

"I'm not sure you'd like the real me," Daniel said. "I'd rather have you see the *perfect* me."

"I don't want a perfect man," Phoebe told him. "I just want someone I can talk to and someone who cares about me."

"I can be both of those," Daniel said. "But I'm still going to try to make tonight perfect for you." He took her hand and led her through the apartment to the living room couch. A fire glowed in the fireplace, and Daniel had draped the coffee table with a silky scarf. A bottle of champagne sat chilling in an ice bucket, and a fondue pot with melted chocolate was next to it. Spread out on a platter nearby were a bunch of gigantic red strawberries.

"Strawberries," Phoebe said, a rush of disappointment shooting through her.

"Don't they look amazing? I went to two different farmers' markets to find the best ones," Daniel said.

"They do look beautiful," Phoebe said ruefully. "I just can't eat them."

"What? Why not?"

"I'm allergic." Phoebe breathed in the scent of the melted chocolate. "I can still eat this, though!"

"I can't believe you're allergic to strawberries," Daniel cried, panicked. "I thought they were totally safe! I mean, peanuts or something I could understand. But it never occurred to me that strawberries could be bad. I'm such an idiot!"

Phoebe stared at him, shocked. "It's no big

deal. You can dip anything in chocolate and it will taste good. I can just stick a spoon in there and eat the chocolate straight."

But Daniel was pacing up and down the room, his face pale. He didn't even seem to be listening to her.

"I'm just sorry you went to so much trouble for nothing," Phoebe added. She reached for his hand. "We can still have a lovely dessert."

"No. It's all ruined," Daniel cried. "It was supposed to be chocolate-dipped strawberries and champagne. They go together. They're romantic. It's a package deal! I don't know what to do now."

Phoebe didn't want to smile when he was so clearly upset. But she couldn't help thinking how sweet it was that he was so intent on making things perfect for her. "Let's just sit down and have some champagne," she suggested.

But Daniel yanked his hand away. "No. I won't . . . I won't know what to say."

"What to say?" Phoebe repeated. "About what?"

"Anything!" Daniel cried. "You have to go."

"Excuse me?" Phoebe asked.

"Sorry. I just . . . I don't mean to be rude. But it's all wrong. We have to reschedule. How's tomorrow night?"

"Um, it's fine," Phoebe said, confused. "But I'd rather just continue with our date tonight."

"No. It will all be off and I'll look stupid."

Daniel strode to the apartment door and pulled it open. "Please."

"I really don't care about the strawberries," Phoebe protested.

Daniel didn't answer.

Phoebe stared at him for a moment. He wouldn't even make eye contact. He was sweating, and his breathing was so fast that she wondered if he was about to hyperventilate. "Okay," she finally said. She picked up her bag and headed for the door. "Good night." She reached up for a kiss, but Daniel started and backed away.

Sadly, Phoebe stepped out into the hall.

"Sorry," he said again, closing the door.

By the time she got back to Halliwell Manor, Phoebe's sadness had turned to annoyance. How could Daniel be so sweet and understanding some of the time, and so bizarrely rude at other times? And why did she still like him so much? She barely even knew him!

"I'm so mad," she announced as she walked into the house. Piper and Paige were standing in the foyer, and a magical white light was just dissipating.

"You're mad?" Piper cried. "My husband just stood me up for dinner—again!"

"Yikes," Phoebe said. "What happened this time?"

"Kerria called him, and he *had* to go," Piper said bitterly.

"Well, he does have to go if one of his charges calls him," Paige pointed out gently.

"This girl calls him every twenty seconds," Piper snapped. "Just because she can't tie her shoes by herself is no reason to ruin my marriage. Leo needs to learn how to say no."

"It sounds like his charge has to learn to set boundaries," Phoebe said. "Can't Leo ask the Elders for help? Isn't there, like, a backup Whitelighter or something?"

"I don't care if there is or not," Piper said. "This is the third time I've gotten all psyched for a date only to be disappointed by my own husband. In the meantime, I'm doing everything around here with Wyatt. It's not fair. This isn't how marriage was supposed to be."

"Does Leo know how upset you are?" Phoebe asked.

"Yes. He says it's all just temporary," Piper sighed. "That our anniversary is just a day and we have to look at the big picture. But I don't care. I need some romance in my life or I'm going to go crazy!"

"Romance is overrated," Phoebe mumbled.

"What happened?" Paige asked.

"Daniel got weird again. He bought us strawberries for dessert."

"You can't eat those," Piper said.

"I know. And it's no biggie, right?" Phoebe replied. "But he flipped out. Said everything was ruined and we couldn't go on with our date."

Paige let out a low whistle. "That settles it. He's a control freak."

"Big-time," Piper agreed.

"You think?" Phoebe asked.

"You show up at his door when he's not expecting you, he can't deal. You say you're allergic to the food he wants you to eat, he can't deal." Paige shook her head. "He obviously can't deal with anything unexpected."

"Which means he needs to control everything around him," Piper added. "To keep the unexpected from happening."

Phoebe headed into the living room, followed by her sisters. "I wish he would just relax. He doesn't need to do anything other than sit there and talk to me. He's so amazing when he's not being weird."

Piper and Paige exchanged glances. "But he's weird a lot," Piper said. "I don't understand why you put up with it."

"Yeah, it's not like you," Paige said.

Phoebe shrugged and plopped down on the couch. "I just like him. Even when he was freaking out tonight, I thought it was kinda sweet. He just wanted things to be perfect for me. It's romantic."

"You don't seem to think it's sweet now," Piper commented.

"That's true." Phoebe frowned. "I wonder what changed?"

"Just cut your losses," Paige suggested. "Forget about Weird Boy and move on."

But the idea of never seeing Daniel again made Phoebe's stomach feel like a rock in her belly. He was so nice, and cute, and . . . well . . . she couldn't define it, exactly. Whenever she saw him, there was just something compelling about him. "I don't want to give up on him," she said. "What if I planned an entire date for tomorrow? Do you think that would work?"

Piper raised an eyebrow. "You still want to date this guy?"

"Yeah. And if I did all the planning, then he wouldn't feel as if he had to control it, right?" Phoebe said. "It would all be done for him."

"I'm not sure it works that way," Paige said.

"But I'll just tell him that's what I'm doing." Phoebe felt herself getting more and more excited as she thought about it. Her face felt hot, and she pulled off her blazer to cool down. "I'll say it's all on me and he doesn't have to do a thing. Then he can just relax and stop trying to make everything perfect. Maybe he'll even be able to open up and tell me about himself for a change."

"He might feel even more out of control that way," Piper said.

Phoebe sneezed. "I don't think so. He really likes me, he's always telling me that. He should trust me to take control for one night." She sneezed again. "Is there some new scented candle in here?"

"No." Paige's eyes were worried. "Do you feel sick?"

"Not really." Phoebe stood up. "I'm just so exhausted all of a sudden. And it's hot in here."

Piper and Paige both glanced down at the sweaters they were wearing. "No, it isn't," Piper said.

"Well, I'm hot." Phoebe sneezed. "I'm going to bed."

"Phoebes? Are you sure you don't have a cold?" Paige asked nervously. "My spell cured Leo this morning, but maybe it's still not working right."

"Don't be silly," Phoebe said. "I feel fine."

Chapter 5

"I feel awful," Phoebe said the next evening as she rummaged through Paige's closet looking for some shoes to borrow. "Do you think Absinthe has chicken soup on the menu?"

"Why . . . you . . . anyway?" Paige replied.

"What?" Phoebe asked. "I'm so stuffed up, I can't hear anything."

"Why don't you just cancel with Daniel tonight? You won't have fun if you feel sick, anyway," Paige yelled.

"No way. I'm going and we'll have a beautiful, romantic night." Phoebe coughed, spinning away from the closet so she didn't infect her sister's entire wardrobe. "Do you think I can wear pumps with this skirt, or do I need boots?"

Paige grabbed a pair of cowboy boots from her closet and thrust them at Phoebe. "Wear these," she said loudly. "I'm sorry I got you sick!"

"What's with that spell of yours, anyway?" Phoebe asked, sitting on the bed to pull on the boots.

Paige bit her lip. "I don't know. It keeps backfiring. Can you imagine if a vanquishing potion for a demon worked this way? One demon is vanquished, and another pops up a few hours later?"

"Maybe one of the ingredients went bad." Phoebe stood up, cringing as pain stabbed through her head. Nothing she took was going to help this sinus headache.

"Maybe. I should check them all," Paige said. "Otherwise . . . worrying . . . powers are on the fritz."

Phoebe squinted at her sister, trying to read Paige's lips since she couldn't exactly hear the words.

Paige shook her head. "You shouldn't go tonight."

"I'm going." Phoebe checked her hair in the mirror, then headed for the stairs. She was determined to have one good date with Daniel, no matter what.

Sucking on a cough drop, she drove over to his apartment. She had it planned down to the tiniest detail: First she would sit him down and explain that she'd taken over the perfect-date responsibility for the evening. Then they would go to Absinthe, where she would order for them both so that Daniel didn't have to worry. Then they would go over and take a walk along Alamo Square. And then they would go back to Daniel's and she would simply kiss him good night and leave. There was no room for a Daniel freak-out anywhere in there. It was just a simple, elegant date.

With lots of sneezing and coughing, she thought ruefully.

Phoebe trudged up the stairs to Daniel's door. To her surprise, it was open.

"Hello?" she called. "Daniel?"

Voices drifted out from the kitchen. Phoebe hesitated on the doorstep. Should she go in, or would that throw Daniel off?

" . . . kinda have to go now," she heard him say.

"But where am I?" a woman's voice asked.

That's it. I'm going in, Phoebe decided. She headed for the kitchen, and stopped short when she saw the woman at the table. The old woman at the table. She had white hair in a bun, an apron that said "Williams Market" on it, and a baffled look on her face.

"Um, hi," Phoebe said.

Daniel turned to her, relieved. "Hi, Phoebe," he said. "I'm glad you're here."

"What's going on?" she asked.

"I'm not entirely sure," Daniel replied. "This is Olive."

"Hello, dear," the old lady said.

"Hi, Olive." Phoebe sat down at the table

across from her. "Are you a relative of Daniel's?"

"Oh, no. I don't even know him," Olive said pleasantly.

Phoebe looked at Daniel, who shrugged. "Olive followed me home from the store."

"I work as a greeter at Williams Market," Olive said. "Three nights a week. It gets me out of the house."

"That's great," Phoebe told her. "But . . . why did you follow Daniel home?"

"Well, that's what I'm trying to figure out, dear," Olive said. "I said good night to him as he was leaving—that's what greeters do, you know. We say hello and good-bye."

Phoebe leaned forward, trying to hear better. Olive wasn't talking very loudly, and Phoebe's head was still stuffed up. "I'm sorry, you said good night to him?"

"Yes. And he said it back. He's a very polite young man."

Phoebe smiled up at Daniel. "I know. But how did you end up here?"

"He said good night, and I just found myself following him." Olive looked as confused as Phoebe felt.

"Didn't you notice her following you?" she asked Daniel.

"I was on the phone," he said. "My cell rang just as I was leaving the market, and by the time I hung up I was home. And she was right behind me."

"All I remember was that I thought he was such a nice boy and I was listening to him talk to his friend," Olive said. "But I'm not even sure where I am. I didn't mean to leave my post at the market."

"We're not far away," Daniel told her. "Your store is just around the block."

"Do you want us to walk you there?" Phoebe asked.

"Oh no, sweetheart, I can walk around a block." Olive chuckled.

Phoebe didn't know what to make of it. The congestion in her head made everything seem unreal, and she wondered if maybe she'd gotten a fever and started hallucinating. "Olive, have you ever done this before?" she asked.

"Certainly not!" Olive cried. "That's what's so odd about it. But I suppose you two want to be alone now. What a lovely couple you are."

She stood up and moved slowly toward the door. Phoebe couldn't see anything physically wrong with the woman, and she didn't seem incoherent. Simply a little confused. And a little reluctant to leave. She stood at the apartment door, beaming at them.

"We're happy to walk you back to work," Phoebe offered again.

"No, no, I'll be fine," Olive said. "What a nice young man." Finally, she turned and left.

Phoebe glanced at Daniel, and they both laughed. "What was *that*?" Phoebe asked.

"I have no idea," he said. "I must just be irresistible to women. I don't even have to try."

"Yeah," Phoebe replied. She knew he was joking, but suddenly it didn't seem that funny. He *was* kind of irresistible, and even she wasn't sure why.

"I thought . . . hand-tossed margarita pizza," Daniel said. "I . . . market getting fresh tomatoes."

"Huh?" Phoebe asked. "I'm sorry. I have such a cold, I'm not hearing well."

"Poor baby," he cried, raising his voice. "You didn't have to come tonight if you felt sick."

"I wanted to. I have the perfect night planned for us," Phoebe told him. "I know you feel pressured to make everything wonderful for me, so tonight I'm going to make everything wonderful for you. We have reservations at Absinthe in twenty minutes."

"But I'm making pizza," Daniel said.

"What?"

"Pizza. I already started on the crust." Daniel gestured into the kitchen.

"I don't want pizza," Phoebe said. "I made reservations. I had to call in two favors to get us a table there. It will be romantic."

"I was planning on eating here," Daniel argued. "I'm making pizza."

"I know," Phoebe snapped. "You already said that."

"Sorry. I thought maybe you didn't hear me."

"I heard you. But I made the plans for tonight," she said. "I want to give you a break from planning. It's not fair that you do all the work for our dates."

Daniel took a deep breath, but he looked alarmed. "That's sweet of you, Phoebe, but it's not necessary."

"It's no problem. We should go," she said, standing up. "I don't want to be late."

"I'd rather stay here," Daniel protested.

Phoebe felt a wave of annoyance. This was supposed to be their big romantic date and it was already going wrong. "Why?" she asked. "Can't you just let me take over for tonight?"

"But you're sick," Daniel told her. "Wouldn't you be more comfortable here than in some crowded restaurant?"

"No," she said.

"I already started cooking, though," he pointed out.

Phoebe glanced at the counter. Raw pizza dough was laid out on a stone slab. Nothing had been cooked yet at all. Daniel was fidgeting, rocking from one foot to the other and looking nervous.

Between her aching head, the strange woman from the market, and Daniel's refusal to go to the restaurant, everything seemed fraught with weirdness. Daniel didn't have a good reason for staying in, Olive didn't have a good reason for following him home, and

Phoebe suddenly realized that she didn't have a good reason for even wanting to go out with Daniel again in the first place.

"You know what?" she said. "I do feel sick. I'm going home."

"But what about our date?" he asked.

She studied his face. He didn't even look as cute as he used to. Phoebe usually had a hard time saying good-bye to Daniel, but right now it seemed easy. "Sorry," she told him. Then she walked out without a backward glance.

"Maybe I should add some eucalyptus leaf to help with the congestion," Paige said an hour later.

Phoebe just moaned. She'd been sitting at the kitchen table with her head on her arms ever since she got home from Daniel's.

"You don't need to put that in a potion," Piper said, grabbing the dried eucalyptus leaves from Paige. "I'll just put it in a bowl of boiling water and Phoebe can steam away her congestion."

Phoebe lifted her heavy head and blinked at her sisters. "Something's wrong," she croaked.

"I know. You have a whopper of a cold," Paige replied. "I'm working on it. I'm going to use all different ingredients, then say the same spell. If it works, that means one of my old ingredients was faulty. If it doesn't work, it means the vanquishing spell itself is faulty."

Phoebe shook her head, then immediately regretted it. "Ow. No, I mean something is wrong with Daniel."

"He's a control freak," Piper said. "Just like we told you."

"He's a control *super*freak," Paige corrected her. "Can't even let you make the plans for one night."

"It's more than that," Phoebe said. "I can't put my finger on it. But that thing with the old lady was bizarre."

"I can't argue with that," Piper replied, setting the kettle on the stove to boil some water.

"Did Daniel think it was as strange as you did?" Paige asked.

"I couldn't tell," Phoebe admitted. "But I got a weird vibe from him as soon as I walked in the door. Usually as soon as I see him, I'm happy. I find him so attractive. Tonight I didn't, not as much."

"You didn't, but Olive did," Paige cracked.

"Are you saying you think he's got some kind of power?" Piper asked. "Something supernatural?"

Phoebe groaned and dropped her head back onto her arms. "I'm not sure what I'm saying."

"I've never met the guy," Paige put in. "But he doesn't sound like your type. And yet you've been willing to give him one chance after another to get things right with you. You're not usually that patient."

"Thanks," Phoebe mumbled.

"You think maybe he put a love spell on himself or something?" Piper asked. "Something that attracted not only Phoebe, but also Olive from the store."

"And a couple of brawling alley cats," Phoebe added. "Oh, and Ryan, my assistant."

"Powerful spell," Paige said.

"You said he doesn't like to talk about himself," Piper mused. "So all we really know about him is that he has some kind of magnetism. I guess that could be from a love spell."

"If it is, it doesn't sound too dangerous," Paige said.

"That's true. But anybody who fools around with magic could be a threat to us," Piper replied. "Who knows what his real agenda is? Plenty of people have set traps for us before."

"So what should we do?" Phoebe asked.

"*You* should spend ten minutes steaming and then go to bed," Piper said, pouring the hot water into a bowl with eucalyptus leaves and setting it in front of Phoebe. Paige tossed her a small towel, and Phoebe bent over the steam. "*I* will spend tomorrow following Daniel. We'll see what he does when he's not busy trying to impress you."

Piper leaned back against the wooden slats of the park bench and yawned. A quick glance to her side showed her Wyatt asleep in his stroller.

"Lucky boy," she murmured. A nap sounded good right about now.

Daniel had been sitting on a park bench ten feet away from her for the past half hour, reading a book on event planning. He hadn't moved or even looked up once. If he was some kind of supernatural baddie, he was the most boring one ever.

And he wasn't even as cute as she'd thought he was when she saw him speak at the museum gala. Why was Phoebe so attracted to him? Why were all those other people—and animals?

Piper pulled out her cell and dialed Paige. "How long do I have to stay here?" she asked when her sister answered the phone.

"You've only been gone for an hour," Paige replied.

"He's the most unremarkable guy on the planet," Piper complained.

"We agreed that you would follow him all day."

"I don't get the impression that he's planning to move," Piper said. An electronic merengue tune sounded, and Daniel jumped. He put down the book and searched in his backpack for a cell phone.

"He's finally doing something. I'll call you back," Piper told Paige. She hung up and positioned her own book so that she could watch Daniel while looking as if she were reading.

"Hello?" he said into his cell. "Why didn't

you call me right back?" His expression was anxious, and his big blue eyes searched the park.

Piper squinted at him. She hadn't realized he had such nice eyes.

"But it was a complete disaster," Daniel was saying. "I'm not even sure what happened."

Poor guy, thought Piper. *He really sounds upset.*

Daniel suddenly jumped to his feet and took off down the path. Surprised, Piper shoved her book in the diaper bag, grabbed Wyatt's stroller, and followed him.

" . . . keeps doing things I don't expect," Daniel was saying. "But I remembered everything you told me. I didn't panic. I stayed calm and tried to talk her into doing the stuff I had planned. She just left anyway."

He's talking about Phoebe, Piper realized. *About last night.*

"It's really bad, man," Daniel went on. "She might never talk to me again. It's not working!" He listened for a moment, then said, "No. I'm not giving up on her! But we've got to try something different."

Phoebe's right, Piper thought. *He is really attractive. It's sweet how upset he is about their bad date.*

"I'm afraid to call her until we have a game plan," Daniel said. "I don't want to mess things up anymore. Can't you come over and practice with me or something? This might be my last chance."

They'd reached the main road leading out of

the park, and Daniel suddenly began jogging to make the light at the intersection. Piper slowed down and sighed. She couldn't run with Wyatt's stroller. "So much for our big day of tailing Daniel," she told her sleeping son.

Her body gave a little shudder as she watched Daniel disappear into the crowd of pedestrians on the sidewalk across the street. She felt as if an invisible hand were trying to tug her after him.

She didn't want him to go. The air felt colder without him nearby.

"He is definitely a keeper," she murmured.

Chapter 6

"**He is** definitely a keeper," Piper said, a big, silly smile on her face. "I'd totally forgotten how good-looking he is."

Phoebe rubbed her bleary eyes and stared at her sister. Piper didn't do big, silly smiles. And she didn't usually care if guys were cute or not. "Is she making any sense at all?" she asked Paige.

"Nope," Paige replied. "None."

"I wondered if it was just my cold," Phoebe said. "Piper, you heard Daniel talking about me with some stranger on the phone."

"He was so upset that things went badly on your date. It was really sweet," Piper said. "He wants to figure out how to do better next time."

"Yeah, because he's trying to seduce her into some evil trap," Paige put in from her perch at the breakfast bar. "Earth to Piper: Discussing their romantic mistakes is not something that normal guys do."

Piper thought about it for a moment. "Maybe not. But it seemed normal at the time."

Phoebe took a sip of tea to clear her throat. Her cold was a killer—and it wasn't getting any better. "What else did he do?"

"He just sat around reading a book for his job and then he was on the phone. Then I lost him," Piper said.

"Did you try to find him again?" Paige asked.

Piper shrugged. "It didn't seem very important. I'd already heard everything I needed to know."

"That he was discussing the best way to deal with Phoebe."

"Yeah. It proved that he's just a good guy who wants to make her happy." Even Piper frowned when she said that. "But it doesn't prove that at all, does it?"

"Nope." Phoebe sighed. "This is what always happens to me with Daniel too. Everything he says seems to make sense and he's such a good guy and he's so cute. . . ."

"But then when you think about it all later, none of it makes sense," Piper finished for her.

"And he doesn't seem like such a good guy based on that phone call," Paige added.

"Last time I saw him, he didn't seem so great, though," Phoebe said, confused. "He didn't even look as good as usual. What's up with that?"

"There's definitely something weird," Paige

said. "Nobody can make Piper go all gooey like this without magic."

"Hey!" Piper cried.

Paige ignored her. "I better take a crack at following him," she continued. "Maybe I'll find out more."

"I found out plenty," Piper protested.

Phoebe looked at her skeptically.

"What?" Piper asked. "I found out that he's going to try to get another date with you. And that he likes to get his romantic advice from some guy on the phone."

"I think we're gonna need a little more to go on than that," Paige said.

"The same thing will happen to you, most likely," Phoebe told her. "You'll just follow him around thinking everything he does is wonderful."

"Maybe I should do some nonfollowing recon," Paige suggested. "Just snoop around his apartment or his office and see what I can find out. If he's not there, he can't put the whammy on me, right?"

"Probably not," Piper said.

"Are we thinking he's got detailed notes of his get-Phoebe plot stashed somewhere?" Phoebe asked.

"Hey, you never know. Some of these baddies are pretty dumb," Paige pointed out.

"We're not even sure he *is* a baddie," Piper said. "But if there's anything supernatural going on, there are usually signs. You should be able to find something in his apartment."

"Tomorrow when he's at work, I'll orb in and play Nancy Drew," Paige promised. "But today, I'm going to vanquish Phoebe's cold."

"It's about time," Phoebe mumbled.

Paige held up a bottle of potion. "I used fenugreek instead of the red clover and mugwort—it handles sore throats *and* coughing. And the eucalyptus instead of the chamomile. And astragalus instead of sage and echinacea."

Phoebe wrinkled her nose. "It sounds disgusting."

"You don't have to drink it," Paige told her. "It's a vanquishing potion." She tossed it at Phoebe and said the spell.

Phoebe flinched as the potion bottle exploded on the table in front of her, releasing its magic in a burst. She'd thrown lots of vanquishing potions in her life, but she'd never been the recipient of one until now. It was kind of alarming.

But then the potion rose into the air, briefly surrounding her head before it disappeared. "It smells good," she said. "Hey! I can smell!" She took a deep breath and smiled. She hadn't been able to take a deep breath in days. Her throat didn't hurt, her eyes didn't feel irritated, and she suddenly realized she could hear a sound all the way from upstairs. "I can hear again!" she said happily. "Wyatt's crying."

Piper listened for a second, then jumped up

and headed for the stairs. "Looks like you're cured," she called over her shoulder. "I couldn't even hear that!"

Phoebe leaned back in her chair, just enjoying the sensations of being healthy again. "We should bottle that and sell it," she joked.

But Paige wasn't smiling. "Let's just see if it really works this time. Otherwise I'm gonna have to take a class in remedial spell casting!"

"Paige!" Phoebe yelled on Monday morning. "Paige!"

Paige sat up in bed and yawned. "What?" she called. Her door opened, and Phoebe appeared, all dressed for work.

"Aren't you going to Daniel's today?" Phoebe asked.

"Yeah." Paige blinked at her sister sleepily. "Why?"

"It's almost ten o'clock," Phoebe said. "You should get going."

"Geez, anxious much?" Paige mumbled, climbing out of bed. "I wanted to give him time to leave for work. Not everybody goes in at eight a.m., you know. Look at you."

"I stayed up late working last night," Phoebe protested. "I deserved an extra hour of sleep."

Paige raised her eyebrows.

"I just want to know what the deal is with Daniel," Phoebe admitted. "It's freaking me out that he was talking about me yesterday. If there's a trap for me, I'd rather know it right away. Can you go now?"

"Okay, okay, I'm going," Paige said. "Give me ten minutes."

Nine minutes later, she was standing in the living room of Daniel's apartment, the white light from her orbing dissipating around her. Paige stood still, listening. The first rule of any good reconnaissance orb was silence. You could never be sure what to expect when orbing into a new place—for all she knew Daniel had a secret roommate whose morning she was about to ruin.

Nothing. No sound except the noise of traffic outside on the street.

Paige relaxed and took a look around. The place was spotless. "Looks like you were lying about your slobbiness, Mr. Daniel Lemond," she murmured. This wasn't just casual tidiness. This was neat-freak cleanliness. "Unusual for a guy," Paige said. "But not supernatural."

She headed straight for the bedroom. If he was hiding any evil paraphernalia, it would probably be in there. He couldn't very well leave it sitting around in the kitchen or living room if Phoebe was coming over for dates.

Pushing open the door, she stepped into the darkened room. The bed was neatly made, and the blinds were drawn. Paige flicked on the overhead light, but it didn't show anything more remarkable than a wooden dresser and a comfy chair in the corner. She pulled open the closet door and glanced at the rows of matching hangers with dress shirts and pants lined up on the top bar. Jeans and pullovers were stacked on the shelves nearby.

"No spell books in here," Paige commented. "No crystals, candles, or sacrificial knives, either." It was just the normal closet of a normal guy. She did a quick check of the shoe rack and the tie caddy. Nothing.

The bathroom cabinet was filled with the usual assortment of pain medications and toiletries. No potion bottles or vials of blood or whatever else evil people kept in their medicine chests.

"What is your deal, Daniel?" Paige asked as she headed back toward the living room. "Could you really be just a cute control freak who talks to his friends about how to impress Phoebe?"

She wandered over toward a huge aquarium built into the wall behind the couch. A giant, bright orange fish with horns growing from its head swam lazily around the corals inside. Paige tapped on the glass and the fish came toward her, so she bent down to take a closer look. It was gorgeous. But it wasn't a clue to any evil behavior on Daniel's part.

She straightened up with a sigh—and found herself gazing into the glowing yellow eyes of a demon.

Paige froze. The demon was reflected in the glass of the aquarium. It stood behind her, looking over her shoulder.

She spun around, automatically raising her arm to throw a fireball.

The living room was empty.

Nothing was out of place, and nothing was moving. There was no demon. There was no hint of magic in the air, no shimmering, nothing.

Paige whirled back to look at the aquarium, but the only things reflected in the glass now were the couch and the TV. No yellow eyes. No demon.

She ran into the attached kitchen and looked around. No demon. Slowly, she relaxed. The apartment was demon free.

But had there ever been a demon there at all?

Paige leaned against the kitchen counter and thought about it. What kind of demon just vanished without a trace? And what kind of a demon wouldn't at least attempt to kill her before he disappeared?

She tried to remember what it had looked like, but she'd only gotten a split-second glimpse before it took off. Had she just imagined the whole thing?

Uneasy, Paige decided to leave the apartment, demon or no demon. She orbed back home. Piper was in Wyatt's room, changing his diaper with one hand and holding a tissue over her nose and mouth with the other.

"Wow, it smells *that* bad?" Paige cracked.

Piper shot her an icy look. "I hab a colb," she said.

"Huh?"

"A *colb*," she said.

"Oh." Paige winced. "Sorry. Let me take Wyatt." She finished up his diaper, picked him up, and put him into the crib for his nap. Piper retreated to the door of the room, still holding the tissue.

"I don't want to get him sick again," she said as Paige joined her in the hall. They left the door open a tiny bit and headed downstairs.

"You got me sick," Piper said accusingly. "You cured Phoebe and gave it to me."

Paige groaned. "That means it's the spell. I changed all the ingredients in the vanquishing potion."

Piper sneezed. "But the spell sounds fine," she said. "It should work."

"Maybe it's me," Paige said slowly. "Do you think there's something wrong with my powers?"

"I don't know," Piper replied. "Are you having any other problems?"

"Not really." Paige frowned. "Although I kinda thought I saw a demon at Daniel's apartment."

"What?" Piper cried.

"But I only saw it for a second," Paige said. "I may have just imagined it."

"Imagined what?" Phoebe asked. She'd just come in the front door.

"A demon," Paige told her. "In Daniel's living room."

"*What?*" Phoebe's face paled.

"I'm not sure," Paige said quickly. "I was looking at his fish tank and I thought I saw a demon reflected in the glass. But when I turned around he was gone. It could've been just a trick of the light."

"What kind of light makes you think you're seeing demons?" Phoebe asked doubtfully.

"I don't know. It is a pretty funny-looking fish." Paige shrugged. "Maybe it gave me ideas. Maybe I'm hallucinating."

Phoebe's mouth was set in a grim line. "I knew there was something evil going on."

"Calm down," Piper told her. "We don't know anything for sure. All we have to go on is the fact that Daniel talks about you on the phone and has a demonic-looking fish."

"Yeah. And aren't you supposed to be at work?" Paige asked.

"I couldn't concentrate," Phoebe said. She strode into the living room and began pacing. "Do you think Daniel is a demon?"

Paige frowned. "If he was, why did I only see him in the glass? He could have attacked me the second I orbed in."

"Besides, he doesn't really strike me as a demon, and I've got pretty good instincts," Piper said. "I've never gotten any kind of demonic vibe from him."

"Neither have I, and I've spent a lot of time with him," Phoebe said. "But why else would there be a demon in his apartment?"

"I keep telling you I'm not sure there was a demon," Paige protested. But Phoebe was already heading for the kitchen. Paige and Piper followed.

Phoebe grabbed the phone and began dialing.

"Who are you calling?" Piper asked.

"Daniel, obviously. If he was at work, then Paige couldn't have seen him in his apartment."

"I'm not sure—" Paige began.

"Shh!" Phoebe held up a finger. "Hi. Daniel Lemond, please." She listened for a moment, her forehead creasing into a frown. "Are you sure? All day? Thank you."

"What? What happened?" Paige asked as her sister hung up the phone.

"The receptionist said Daniel called in sick. He hasn't been there all day." Phoebe's eyes were wide. "Which means he could have been home. . . ."

"And he could have been the demon Paige saw," Piper added.

"*Maybe* saw," Paige said.

"Or he could have been attacked by the demon Paige saw," Phoebe said. "He could be in real danger."

Paige took a deep breath. She still wasn't sure about what she'd seen, but it was obvious what they had to do. She held out her hands to her sisters. "Let's get over to Daniel's place—fast!"

Chapter 7

Phoebe grabbed onto Paige's hand and they orbed into Daniel's living room. Before the light had even faded, Phoebe dropped into a fighting stance. Her eyes darted from one end of the room to the other, checking for enemies.

Everything looked normal. The TV was on, turned to a news channel. The big orange fish was watching them from its aquarium. And Daniel was sitting at the kitchen table, a spoonful of soup halfway to his mouth as he stared at them in surprise.

"Oops," Paige murmured.

"Phoebe?" Daniel croaked, dropping the spoon into his bowl with a clatter.

"Um . . . hi." Phoebe put on a bright smile. "Sorry to just drop in on you like this."

"Anyone see a demon?" Piper whispered behind her.

"I'll check the bedroom. You take the bathroom,"

Paige whispered back. They spread out as Phoebe walked toward the kitchen, trying to act casual.

"Wh-what are you . . . ?" Daniel's voice trailed off.

"I called your office and they said you were at home," Phoebe told him. "We—my sisters and I—we thought you might be in some kind of trouble."

Daniel frowned. "Why would I be in trouble?"

"Oh, just because my sister thought she saw a—um, she thought she saw a creepy guy in your apartment earlier."

"Your sister was watching my apartment?" he asked, alarmed. Then his eyes widened. "Or was she *in* my apartment? Did she come in like you just did?"

Phoebe didn't know what to say, but she had a feeling that the expression on her face told him he was right. "Listen, I know it seems strange. Unbelievable, even. You weren't really supposed to see us do that—"

"So she *was* in my apartment?" Daniel interrupted. "Why?"

Phoebe blinked in confusion. He didn't even seem to care about the orbing part of it. He only seemed to care about . . . well, about the breaking and entering part of it. "Um . . ."

"Nobody in the bathroom," Paige announced, coming back into the room. She held out her hand to Daniel. "Hi, I'm Paige."

His face went red, and he suddenly jumped

up from his chair, almost knocking it over. "Yeah. Hi," he mumbled, not meeting her eyes.

Paige slowly lowered her hand. "Sorry to bother you when you're sick," she said.

"Bedroom's clean." Piper came into the kitchen and sneezed. "And I had to steal a tissue. I hope that's okay."

Daniel backed into the kitchen and began fumbling around with the soup pot, moving it from the stove to the counter and trying not to look at Phoebe or her sisters. "It's fine."

Piper shot Phoebe a questioning look. Phoebe shrugged. "So you're okay, Daniel? Nothing weird is going on?"

"Other than us showing up in your living room," Paige put in.

"No, nothing weird." Daniel still didn't look at any of them. Normally Phoebe would have thought he was flipping because they'd materialized out of thin air. But Daniel just seemed kind of embarrassed. He kept dropping the pot as he tried to ladle extra soup into a Tupperware. And his cheeks were fire engine red.

"So you're sick, huh?" Piper asked. "I have a terrible cold myself. What's wrong with you?"

"Uh, I'm not sure."

"You've been home all day?" Phoebe asked.

Daniel just stared at her without answering.

"Has anyone else been here today?" Paige asked him.

"No," he said quickly.

"Are you—"

"Just me. Nobody else," he insisted. He glanced at Phoebe and then quickly looked away. "I'm, uh, it's a mess in here and . . ."

And I'd really like you to leave, Phoebe finished the thought for him. She'd never seen him so uncomfortable. She could hardly blame him. Most people would freak out if three women suddenly appeared in their living room. "Okay, well, since you're all right." She grabbed her sisters and herded them toward the front door. "I'll talk to you later."

Daniel didn't even look at her as she ushered Piper and Paige outside and closed the door.

"Well, that was awkward," Piper said in the hallway.

"I guess we should have orbed out here instead of in there," Paige commented. "Sorry. I was just so worried that there was a demon attacking Daniel. Or something."

"Let's go home," Phoebe said.

Paige orbed them straight to Wyatt's room to check on him. He was still sound asleep, so they tiptoed out of the room and up to the attic.

"I don't get it," Phoebe said. "If Daniel was really home all day, how come Paige didn't see him when she was there?"

"Maybe she did see him. Maybe he was the demon," Piper suggested.

"You guys, I'm seriously not sure there was a demon." Paige threw herself down on one of the old chairs. "Besides, if Daniel was a demon, he would have attacked me."

"And he wouldn't have been so surprised to hear that you were watching his apartment earlier," Phoebe put in. "He's not a demon. It just doesn't feel right."

"I agree," Piper said. "But he was still lying to us. He obviously wasn't home this morning, or Paige would have seen him."

"So he's got some kind of weird attractiveness power and he likes to fake sick," Paige said. "Where does that leave us?"

"He could be in league with the demon," Phoebe guessed.

Paige sighed in frustration. "You know what? I take it back. I didn't see a demon. I saw a weird reflection in a fish tank. That's the only thing that happened. Otherwise, I think Daniel is just a control freak who likes Phoebe."

"And attracts cats and old ladies and Phoebe's straight male assistant," Piper added.

"Well, he didn't attract *me* today," Paige argued.

"He didn't have time to. He hardly even spoke to us," Phoebe said. "But you know what's weird? I didn't get the impression that it was the orbing that freaked him out. He didn't seem that fazed by it."

Piper sneezed. "Sorry, guys, I have to go take a decongestant and lie down. Phoebes, maybe you should just forget about Daniel. He doesn't seem like a threat to us."

"Yeah, and now that you look like a crazy magical stalker, he might decide he doesn't want another chance with you after all," Paige said brightly.

Phoebe gave her a half smile. "Thanks."

She sighed. No matter what her sisters said, she couldn't help feeling there was something else going on. Why hadn't Daniel been more concerned about them orbing into his apartment? Why had he lied about being home all day? Whenever she thought about the great, sweet, funny guy she'd fallen for, she couldn't help wanting to be with him again. How could that amazing man be involved in anything evil?

When she woke up the next day, Phoebe was still thinking about Daniel. She glanced at her clock—seven thirty. There was plenty of time to swing by Daniel's place before work. Maybe she could just go over and check it out on her own. Her sisters hadn't found out anything very conclusive by following Daniel. She might do better.

But when she pulled up in front of Daniel's building, Phoebe wasn't sure what to do. She couldn't orb inside, like Paige. And she couldn't very well follow him around unless he came out. *Maybe I'll just go knock on the door*, she thought. He might flip out like he did the last time she showed up unannounced. Still, she kind of owed him an explanation for yesterday.

Phoebe jumped out of the car and ran up to the door before she could change her mind. When she came to Daniel's apartment, she raised her hand to knock—and heard angry voices from inside.

Frowning, she leaned in to hear better.

" . . . made a total fool of myself!" Daniel was saying. "I wasn't expecting them. And her sisters are just as pretty as she is. I could barely get a single word out."

"Did you tell Phoebe you'd call her?" a guy's voice asked.

Phoebe pressed her ear against the door. Was this who Daniel had been talking to on the phone when Piper followed him?

"No. I didn't say anything," Daniel replied.

"I can't help you win Phoebe over if you keep panicking like this," the other guy said, his voice thin and squeaky.

"Maybe I should just face facts. She's out of my league," Daniel said glumly.

A warm feeling spread through Phoebe's body. Daniel was so sweet! What kind of guy would spend so much time thinking about his relationship with her? And talk it over with his friends? It was really cute.

"That's why you have me to help you," the other guy said. "Besides, we have a deal."

A deal? Phoebe thought.

"I need your help as much as you need mine," the guy went on. "And that means that you have to get Phoebe. No matter what it takes."

I've heard enough, Phoebe thought. She didn't know who this squeaky-voiced guy was or what he had to do with Daniel. But she did know that his interest in her was not healthy. She took a step back, stared at the door, and said, "Powers of earth, do not ignore me. Remove this barrier from before me."

A shock wave ran from the top of the door to the bottom, then the entire thing swung inward.

Phoebe leaped through as the two men inside turned to her in surprise. Daniel's mouth dropped open. And the demon was so shocked that he jumped straight into the air.

Demon! Phoebe's fighting instincts kicked in immediately and she dropped into a ready stance.

She stared at the demon. He was covered in little bumps that looked like warts, and his skin had a purplish tinge. His eyes blazed yellow as he stared at her. But when she raised her leg to deliver a roundhouse kick at him, he ran backward with a little shriek.

"Phoebe, stop!" Daniel gasped.

"It's a demon," she cried. "It's evil."

"No, it isn't." Daniel stepped in front of the demon. Phoebe had to admit that the thing didn't look too scary cowering behind the love seat. Still, a demon was a demon.

"Daniel, I have to vanquish it," she said.

He paled. "Vanquish? You mean kill him?"

"Yes." Phoebe stepped around him, and the demon let out a whimper.

"Stop her. Don't let her hurt me," it cried.

Phoebe rolled her eyes. "What kind of self-respecting demon whines like that?"

"Daniel," the demon whined.

"You can't kill him," Daniel told her. He took Phoebe's hands in his and stared into her eyes. "He's perfectly nice. His name is Indar. He's a good friend of mine."

"He is?"

"Yes." Daniel smiled gently. "I can't let you hurt him, Phoebe."

She stared at him for a moment. Something didn't seem right about this. But Daniel sounded so reasonable. "I'm supposed to vanquish demons," she said uncertainly.

"But I know him. He's not evil."

She glanced at Indar. His yellow eyes darted from side to side as if he were looking for an escape route. He didn't look especially evil, now that Daniel pointed it out. He was way too pathetic to be evil.

"Can't you just leave him alone?" Daniel asked.

Phoebe nodded. "Well, I guess so. As long as you're sure he's completely harmless."

"I am."

Indar grinned, revealing a set of tiny brownish teeth.

Phoebe turned away from him, feeling a little grossed out. "I'd better go," she said, heading for the door. "You guys have fun."

"Thanks, Phoebe," Daniel called after her.

"Sure thing," she said cheerfully, closing the door on the demon.

Chapter 8

"You *what*?" Paige squeaked ten minutes later in the attic of Halliwell Manor.

"Well, he was really pathetic." Phoebe glanced back and forth between her sisters. "And Daniel said they were friends. His name is Indar."

"Phoebe, it was a demon." Piper sneezed, then kept right on lecturing her. "I don't care what its name was. Daniel just stood there and told you that he's in league with a demon—"

"*Friends* with a demon," Phoebe protested. But even that didn't sound quite right.

"—and you said 'great, good for you' and left without vanquishing it," Piper went on. "Have you lost your mind?"

"But Daniel said Indar isn't evil."

Phoebe's words stayed in the air for a moment as her sisters gazed at her in astonishment. "Wow," she finally said. "I sound crazy. I really do." She pushed back her chair, got up, and stalked over to the Book of Shadows.

"What are you doing?" Paige asked.

"Looking up Indar." Phoebe flipped through the old, yellowing pages searching for a picture of the little purple wimp.

"Well, don't lose my place," Paige told her. "I'm trying to find a healing spell to replace the cold-vanquishing spell I wrote." She pointed to the bowl of hot water on the trunk in front of Piper. "Steam," she commanded.

Piper bent over the bowl of steamy water and pulled a towel over her head.

"I've never seen a demon be such a wuss before," Phoebe told them. "Too bad there's not a section for cowardly demons."

"You know, I'm not convinced Indar is the only problem here," Piper said from under her towel.

"What do you mean?" Phoebe asked.

"I mean that Indar didn't tell you not to vanquish him. Daniel did."

"So?"

"So Daniel announced that he was pals with a demon and the demon wasn't evil and you shouldn't kill it," Paige put in. "And you agreed."

Piper peeked out from one corner of the towel. "And then you came home here and told us about it like it was the most normal thing in the world."

"It made sense at the time," Phoebe tried to

defend herself. "Daniel sounded perfectly reasonable. And Indar was acting like such a baby that he didn't seem threatening."

"Right. And Piper thought it made sense that Daniel was discussing your relationship in great detail on the phone. And the old lady from the market thought it made sense to follow Daniel home," Paige said.

Phoebe looked up from the book. "So what does that mean?"

"It means there has to be a reason that Daniel can keep talking you into going out with him again even when he acts like a jerk," Piper said. "And if he's hanging out with a demon, it's probably because the demon is using him. Giving him powers of persuasion or something."

"Maybe Indar wasn't such a coward after all," Phoebe said slowly. "Maybe he was only acting that way to keep me from fighting him. Meanwhile he was using poor Daniel to tell me everything was okay."

"Things just sound more convincing when they're coming from the mouth of a cute guy." Paige sighed.

"I can't believe I didn't vanquish that stupid demon when I had the chance," Phoebe said, sounding determined. "I'm going to go back there and do it now. Paige?"

"Hold on," Piper said, sitting up with her face flushed from the steam. "If you go back there, the same thing will just happen again—Indar will use Daniel to make you stop. We've got to get Indar on his own."

"So let's summon him here." Paige immediately began flipping through the Book of Shadows for a summoning spell.

"We have to find out what he's been doing to Daniel before we vanquish him," Phoebe said. "If Daniel is an Innocent and Indar put some kind of spell on him, we need to know how to reverse the damage."

"Let's use this one," Paige said. "If Indar did a spell or left some kind of talisman at Daniel's place, it will summon that, too." Phoebe and Piper got up and read over her shoulder:

> *Source of magic, heed our cry.*
> *From Daniel's home, let your power fly.*
> *We summon you before us three,*
> *Secret enchantment, hear our plea.*

A magic wind blew through the attic, rustling the pages of the Book of Shadows. Then a shimmering bubble appeared in the middle of the room, distorting their view of everything within it. A figure came into view, hard to see through the warping of the bubble.

"I think I'll pop that thing," Phoebe said. She strode over and stuck her finger into the bubble. It vanished with a loud puckering sound, and Phoebe found herself standing face-to-face with Daniel.

"Daniel!" she cried.

"Phoebe?" he said. He looked frantically around the room. "Where am I?"

"In my attic," she told him.

"What am I doing here?"

"That's what we'd like to know." Piper approached, arms crossed over her chest. "We were expecting your demon friend."

Daniel's eyes flew to Phoebe. "You said you wouldn't hurt him!"

His voice sounded so accusatory that Phoebe felt a sting of guilt as if it were a physical slap. "I know, but . . ."

"That's not the point," Piper cut in. "We did a spell to summon Indar, but instead Daniel showed up. Maybe they are the same person, after all."

"They're not," Phoebe said. "I saw them both at the same time, remember?"

"Then how could Daniel have responded to our spell?" Paige asked.

"Why are you trying to summon Indar if you're not planning to hurt him?" Daniel asked. "I really can't let you do that, Phoebe. He's only trying to help. It wouldn't be fair if he got vanquished in return."

Phoebe found herself listening, enrapt, as Daniel spoke. Paige stood nearby, smiling at him. But Piper's eyes were flashing with anger. "He's trying to *help*?" she repeated skeptically. "Trying to help you trap Phoebe, you mean? I heard you talking on the phone to him. You kept saying you were going to get her."

"Yeah. Get her to be my girlfriend," Daniel said. His cheeks turned almost maroon. "I said I was going to get her to like me," he finished softly.

"Awww," Phoebe and Paige said together.

Piper shot them a look. "What is with you two?" she asked. "We summoned the source of magic and he showed up. You shouldn't be cooing at him."

That made sense. Phoebe knew it made sense. But she still couldn't stop thinking that Daniel was the sweetest thing in the world. She shook her head, trying to think logically. "But he's not a demon. He's human," she said.

"And he's not trying to attack us or anything," Paige added.

"He's also not particularly weirded out by the fact that he's standing in our house because we drew him here with a spell," Piper pointed out. "And he hangs around with demons. And he obviously has some bizarre power over the two of you."

"That's not fair," Phoebe argued. "You liked him too when you were following him."

"You were following me?" Daniel asked.

"That's true." Piper frowned. "So why don't I like him now?"

"I'm not even doing anything!" Daniel cried. "Why shouldn't you like me?"

"There's no reason," Phoebe assured him. Paige nodded happily, gazing at Daniel as if he were an adorable puppy.

"You talked my sister out of vanquishing a demon who was standing right in front of her!" Piper said. "A demon who you're clearly in league with, and who is helping you with a plot to get Phoebe. Why *should* I like you?"

Phoebe had to admit that Piper had a point. She turned to Daniel, wondering how he was going to explain himself.

"It's not a plot," he said. And Phoebe believed him immediately. If he said there was no plot, there was no plot.

"Then what is Indar helping you with?" Piper demanded.

"W-with talking," Daniel stammered. "You know . . . romance stuff. Romantic talking."

"Excuse me?" Piper said.

Daniel blew out a frustrated breath, still blushing. "I'm bad at talking. I just . . . I can't talk to women. Especially pretty women. Especially Phoebe."

Phoebe's eyebrows shot up. "What do you mean? We've been dating. We've spent time together. Of course you can talk to me—I've seen you do it."

"Not really." Daniel fidgeted nervously. "Not on my own. I don't, I can't . . . I say dumb things."

"No you don't," Phoebe assured him. "You say sweet things."

"Because Indar tells me to," Daniel said.

"Wait a minute." Paige grabbed Phoebe's arm. "All those times Daniel acted weird, remember? He slammed a door in your face."

"I didn't *slam* it," he said.

But Phoebe suddenly understood what her sister meant. "Every time I did something you weren't planning on, you flipped out," she said to Daniel. "You wouldn't even look at me half the time."

"Or talk to you," Paige put in.

"We thought you were a control freak," Piper said.

"What? No!" Daniel gasped. "I just didn't know what to say!"

"So you blew me off?" Phoebe asked.

"It was better than making a fool of myself," Daniel said miserably. "I didn't want you to see what a total dork I am."

"But you're not a dork. We talked for hours and you were wonderful," she insisted.

"When I made the plans, yes," he said. "Because I would go over every minute of the date with Indar beforehand and he would tell me what to say. So I always knew what to talk about and how to make you like me."

"Because a demon told you how?" Piper asked, one eyebrow raised.

"Yeah."

"Let me get this straight. You have a demon acting as your romantic advisor," Paige said.

"I guess so. I know, I'm a loser." Daniel ran his hand through his hair. "I'm sorry, Phoebe. It's just that you're so perfect and I like you so much. I knew I could never get you on my own. When he offered to help, I thought it would be just what I needed."

"I might have liked you better if you weren't acting like Dr. Jekyll and Mr. Hyde all the time," she told him.

Daniel grimaced. "Sorry. Indar said I was making things worse. I guess he was right."

Phoebe wished she could comfort him—he looked so distraught. And what could be more adorable than a guy who was so desperate to make a good impression on her that he was willing to seek out romantic advice from a demon?

"Listen, I'm . . . uh . . . embarrassed," Daniel said. "Do you guys mind if I use your bathroom? I need to splash water on my face or something."

Phoebe smiled. He'd been furiously blushing since he arrived in the attic—his cheeks probably felt as if they were on fire.

"Downstairs, second door on the left," Piper told him. "But don't try to pull any stunts. We'll find out, and we'll stop you."

Daniel nodded nervously, then inched past her to the attic stairs. He rushed down, avoiding Piper's stare.

"Why are you being so mean to him?" Phoebe asked.

"Because he's probably evil!" Piper cried. "And you're the one he's after. Why are you so calm about it?"

Phoebe frowned. Why *was* she so calm? So what if Daniel said he only wanted to win her heart? He was hanging out with a demon, discussing ways to get into her head.

"Yeah," Paige said suddenly. "Why are we acting like Daniel's a good guy?" She looked as confused as Phoebe felt.

"Wait a minute. My head is all stuffed up," Piper said.

"I know, I know. I'm sorry." Paige rolled her eyes. "I didn't give you the cold on purpose."

"No, I mean I can't hear very well because I'm so congested." Piper turned to Phoebe. "Didn't you have the same symptom when you had this cold?"

"Yes," Phoebe said. "I felt half-deaf."

"Which means you couldn't hear Daniel very well. And that was the day that you got really annoyed with him," Piper said.

"He didn't want to go to Absinthe even though I had reservations," Phoebe remembered. "And he didn't even have a good reason. He just didn't want to go."

"Right. But every other time he acted that way, you totally forgave him and still liked him," Piper pointed out. "That night you couldn't hear him, and you got mad at him."

"Just like you can't hear him too well today,"

Phoebe said, catching on. "And you think he's evil, but Paige and I don't."

"Well, I'm starting to change my mind about that now that he's not here," Paige admitted.

"Exactly," Phoebe said. "But if Daniel was standing here talking to us right now, we'd both think everything he said was completely logical and that he was the nicest guy in the world. Don't you see? It's his voice!"

"That's what I'm thinking." Piper grabbed a tissue from the box she'd been carrying around with her all day. "At least this cold is good for something—it might have helped us figure out what's going on."

"So you think Daniel's voice has some kind of power?" Paige said. "Is that what Indar was really giving him—a vocal love spell to zap Phoebe with?"

"It didn't only work on me, though," Phoebe said. "It worked on you two, and on Ryan, and on the old lady from the store. And I bet on those fighting cats. And probably on every single person at the museum gala, now that I think about it."

"That's some voice," Paige cracked. "Though I don't see how accidentally seducing everybody he comes across is supposed to help Daniel win Phoebe's heart."

"Hang on. We don't think Indar is really trying to be a matchmaker for Daniel and Phoebe, do we?" Piper asked. "He's got to have some ulterior motive, some reason he's helping Daniel."

"Him and Daniel both," Phoebe said. "In fact, I bet Daniel is the real threat. Think about it. We just did a spell to summon the source of magic at Daniel's house—and Daniel's the one who showed up! Not Indar."

Piper sneezed. Paige chewed on her lip, thinking.

"It doesn't make sense, does it?" Phoebe finally said. "How could Daniel be the source of the magic at all? Even if Indar was giving him some kind of voice power along with his romance tips, that would still make Indar the *source* of it."

"Could Daniel be magical just by himself?" Paige asked. "According to him, Indar was telling him what to say, not how to say it."

"He hasn't seemed all that surprised by the magic we've done around him," Piper said thoughtfully. "And he managed to find himself a demon to help him go after Phoebe. Obviously he's no stranger to the supernatural."

"Yeah, where *did* he meet Indar, anyway?" Phoebe said. "It's not like demons advertise their romantic skills in the personal ads."

"I met him after the museum gala," Daniel said from the doorway. They all turned toward him. He looked a little nervous, but calmer than before. "He'd seen me act like an idiot toward you, Phoebe. He said it was obvious that I liked you and that he could help me."

Phoebe felt herself warm toward Daniel immediately. It was so endearing the way he constantly told her how much he liked her.

"That's it." Piper took Daniel's arm and marched him over to an old, overstuffed chair. "You sit down and don't talk. You two, wipe those goofy grins off your faces."

Phoebe glanced at Paige and realized that her half sister had fallen for Daniel's voice power again too. She tried to force her brain to stop reacting to Daniel. Even knowing that some kind of magic was working on her, all she could feel were positive, happy emotions toward him. "Sorry."

"Me too," Paige said.

"What's going on?" Daniel asked.

"Shh!" they all cried.

His brow furrowed in confusion, but Daniel sat back in the chair and kept his mouth shut.

"So a demon walks up to you after the museum gala and says he's going to help you overcome your shyness around Phoebe," Piper said.

Daniel nodded.

"And you didn't think that was the least bit odd?"

"Not—" Daniel began. But a look from Piper shut him up. He just shrugged.

"A demon. Who's purple and ugly," Phoebe put in. "You didn't run away? You just stood there and talked to him?"

Daniel made a few faces, but it was impossible to understand him. Finally he just burst out, "He said he'd help me!"

Paige narrowed her eyes. "Indar isn't the first demon you've seen, is he?"

Daniel shook his head.

"So you hang out with a lot of ugly evil guys?" Phoebe asked.

He shook his head again. "I've seen pictures of demons, but I never met one myself." He sighed. "My mom and my great-aunts used to tell me stories about the demons they fought."

Phoebe's eyebrows shot up. "They fought demons?"

"They said they did. I never saw it."

"Hold on," Piper put in. "Is your mother a witch?"

"She was. She died when I was twelve," Daniel said. "Her whole family always had stories about witches and demons and stuff. I didn't—"

"Quiet!" Piper commanded. Then her tone softened. "Sorry. It's just that when you talk for too long, my sisters lose their good judgment."

"Um . . . what?" Daniel asked.

"Your voice has some kind of power. The only reason it doesn't work on me is that I'm all stuffed up and I can hardly hear you," Piper told him.

"We think Indar 'helped' you by giving you some kind of love spell for your voice," Paige explained.

"I'm not so sure about that," Phoebe said slowly. "Daniel comes from a family of witches. And when we summoned the source of magic, he showed up alone. Maybe that voice power is his own power. Maybe he's a witch."

Daniel laughed, then stopped when he saw Phoebe's serious expression. "I am not," he said.

"Well, why not?" Piper asked. "Obviously you're no stranger to the idea of witches. You must have realized by now that we're witches."

"I guess," Daniel said. "I mean, it's fine with me. I'm not afraid or anything. But I'm not like that. Those are just old stories from my family, demons and powers and magic and stuff."

"Daniel, did you think it was weird when that old lady followed you home from the market?" Phoebe asked.

"A little, I guess."

"Because I thought it was bizarre," Phoebe told him. "But I have a sneaking suspicion that those kinds of things happen to you all the time."

"So what?" He began to blush again. "People like me. Well, except women. I'm too shy to even talk to women. But other people like me enough, I guess. That's normal."

"It's not normal that people like you so much they follow you around," Paige said.

"If I had some kind of power, I wouldn't have all this trouble with women," Daniel argued. "I can't even look at the three of you without getting tongue-tied. And when I really like a woman, like Phoebe, I can't even string two words together." He turned to Phoebe. "You saw how I acted."

"Yeah. You came off as being really rude," she said.

"I did?" He looked horrified.

"Yup. But I liked you anyway," Phoebe told him. "And that's the point. It doesn't even matter what you say. You could be telling me that my butt looks fat in this outfit and I'd still like you because your voice is charmed."

Daniel was shaking his head. "That's crazy."

"No, it isn't." Phoebe stood up and held out her hand to him. "And I'm going to prove it to you."

Chapter 9

"Leo!" Piper yelled as soon as Phoebe had left with Daniel.

Her husband orbed in and took a quick look around. "I'm kinda in the middle of something, honey. Can this wait?"

"No, it can't," Piper retorted.

Leo sighed. "Okay, hang on." He orbed away again.

"Wow." Paige let out a low whistle. "He really is taking you for granted these days, isn't he?"

"So it's not just my imagination?" Piper sighed. "I don't know what to do. He's been spending so much time at work that he's not even acting like himself anymore. I mean, I took care of him when he had the cold. But now that I've got it, he's still away all the time. I have to take care of Wyatt *and* myself. Leo isn't usually that inconsiderate."

"Let me do the cold-vanquishing spell for

you. That will help a little, at least," Paige said.

"It might help me, but it won't help whom-ever the cold jumps to next," Piper replied.

"I'll rework the wording and maybe it won't backfire. That's the only thing I haven't tried yet," Paige said, heading for the stairs.

The attic filled with white light as Leo orbed back in. "Okay, what's wrong?" he asked quickly.

"Does something have to be wrong for me to talk to you?" Piper asked.

"Yes, if you're asking me to leave one of my charges."

"We're your charges too," Paige said from the top of the stairs.

"That's my point. Charges are only supposed to call me if they need me. And that's usually because something's wrong."

Piper felt anger building in the pit of her stomach. Paige took one look at her face and hurried over to stand next to her. "We have a situation," she told Leo. "A demon named Indar and a possible witch named Daniel Lemond."

"Daniel? Phoebe's new boyfriend?" Leo asked.

"His mother and some other relatives were witches, and we think his power is in his voice," Piper said. "But he's been working with this demon to get on Phoebe's good side for some reason—we don't know what. So we're not sure if Daniel is good or evil."

"What do you know about Indar?" Leo asked.

"Not much. He's not in the Book of Shadows," Paige replied.

"Well, I've never heard of any witches named Lemond. I'll have to ask the Elders about that family. But it may take a while," Leo warned them.

"Why?" Piper asked.

He scrubbed his face with his hands. "Kerria is in trouble again. She keeps taking on two and three enemies at a time, and she's not ready for it yet. I don't know if she's ever going to be strong enough for those kinds of fights, in fact. But she keeps getting into them. I have to get back to her."

"This is getting ridiculous," Piper said. "We haven't had any time together in weeks. You haven't even mentioned rescheduling our anniversary dinner."

"I know, honey, I'm sorry," Leo said. "But I have to help her." He gave her a quick kiss on the cheek. "I'll let you know if I find out any information about Daniel."

He orbed away, leaving Piper feeling even worse than before. Her head was pounding, her sister was dating a guy who hung out with demons, and she could hear her son starting to cry through the baby monitor she'd set on the end table.

"You okay?" Paige asked.

Piper sighed. "I'll be better once you do your vanquishing spell on me. I may not be able to control my husband's new charge, but at least I can control my stuffed-up nose!"

"See that guy at the ice-cream place? Go ask him to give you a free waffle cone," Phoebe told Daniel. She pointed across the crowded food court of the mall to a miserable-looking middle-aged guy at an empty booth.

"No way," Daniel said. "Why would he give me something for free?"

"Just do it," she ordered, lightly shoving him in the direction of the ice-cream place. "Oh, ask for mint chip," she added. She loved mint chip.

Daniel reluctantly walked up to the sour-faced ice-cream guy.

"Help you?" the guy asked in a bored tone.

Daniel glanced at Phoebe. "Um, yeah. Can I have a waffle cone, please? Mint chip," Daniel said.

Phoebe nudged him with her elbow.

"And . . . uh . . . can I have it for free?" Daniel added. He took a step back, as if he expected the guy to hit him.

"Sure." The man's entire demeanor had changed. He smiled broadly, grabbed a large waffle cone from a stack behind him, and dug into the mint chip ice cream. "You want two scoops or three?"

Daniel stared at him, shocked.

"Three," Phoebe whispered, nudging Daniel again.

"Three," Daniel said.

"Sure thing. Here you go." The guy handed over the gigantic ice-cream cone. "You have a nice day now."

"Um, thanks. You too." Daniel turned and scurried away, only stopping to give Phoebe the cone when they were around the corner and out of the ice-cream guy's line of sight. "I can't believe he agreed to that," Daniel said.

"He would have agreed to anything you said," Phoebe explained. "Because your voice makes people like you and want to do what you tell them."

"No, not usually," he replied. "You set that up with the ice-cream guy, didn't you?"

Phoebe shook her head as she dug into the ice-cream cone.

"Well, it doesn't prove anything," Daniel grumbled.

"Okay. See that woman near the pet store?" Phoebe nodded toward a harried-looking mom trying to drag her kids away from a puppy in the window.

"Yeah," Daniel said uneasily.

"She's been yelling at her kids for five minutes now. The little boy won't leave until she buys him a puppy, and his sister won't leave until he does."

"Okay."

"If you go over there and tell them to go with their mother, they will," Phoebe said.

Daniel took another look at the kids. The boy was hanging on to a column near the door of the store, refusing to budge as his mom tugged at his arm. The little girl was screeching at the top of her lungs, her eyes screwed shut and her face a deep red color.

"They will not," Daniel said. "They're both in tantrum mode."

"Yes. And you can make them sweet little angels just by talking to them," Phoebe assured him. "Let's go."

Daniel followed her over to the pet store. "Having trouble?" Phoebe asked the mother.

The woman just rolled her eyes. "I should've known better than to walk by a puppy store."

"My friend can help." Phoebe turned to Daniel. "Why don't you have a chat with the kids?"

Embarrassed, Daniel bent down and addressed the screaming girl. "Your mother doesn't like it when you scream like that," he said awkwardly. "Why don't you stop?"

The little girl opened her eyes, shut her mouth, and gave Daniel a big smile.

Surprised, he turned to the boy. "It's time for your family to leave now. Are you going to let go of that column and go with your mother like a good boy?"

The boy dropped his arms from the column and nodded.

The harried woman gazed at Daniel with

wide eyes. "How did you do that?" she asked, a gooey smile spreading across her face.

"Um, I think it's just the novelty of someone they don't know talking to them," he said.

The woman shook her head. "When Stevie gets in a mood like this, *nobody* can ever talk sense into him. That was amazing!"

Daniel shuffled his feet self-consciously. Phoebe could tell that the woman had forgotten all about leaving. She would probably follow Daniel home if she could, just like Olive from the Williams Market.

"Well, glad we could help," Phoebe said. She took Daniel's arm and steered him away. "See what I mean? You have a magic voice."

"That's crazy." Daniel dropped down onto a mall bench. "Don't you think I would have noticed a power like that if I'd had it all my life?"

"Normally I'd say yes," she admitted, sitting next to him. "But the fact that you're so shy means you probably haven't spent much time telling people to do things for you."

"I'm mostly only shy around women. Around you." Daniel stared down at his feet.

"You're not acting shy around me now," she said.

He didn't meet her gaze. "I'm trying to do what Indar told me—just keep talking to you instead of running away. But it's hard. This is embarrassing. It's exactly what I've been try-ing to avoid all this time. I don't know what to say to you, and everything I say is stupid."

"Except it all sounds good to me," Phoebe said. "Because of your voice. You could sit there and sing the alphabet song and I'd probably think you were the coolest guy in San Francisco."

"I doubt it," he muttered.

Clearly, she still hadn't proved her point. "Okay then, see that group of teenagers?" She pointed to some hipster teen guys lounging on a bench nearby, trying to look bored. "Go over there, tell them you just wrote a new song, and then sing them the alphabet."

Daniel was already shaking his head. "I wouldn't have even talked to guys like that in high school," he said. "They're much too cool for me. I'm not going to go make a fool of myself in front of them even if they are ten years younger than I am."

"Trust me, you won't make a fool of yourself," she said. "Go."

With a sigh, Daniel stood and went over to the teenagers. Phoebe watched their faces as he talked to them—at first they looked annoyed, and then while he spoke, they all began to smile like kids seeing Santa Claus. By the time Daniel had finished singing the alphabet, they were all enrapt. They applauded as he walked back over to Phoebe.

She grinned at him. "So? It was a hit, right?"

"I don't understand," Daniel said. "Everybody's acting weird. It's not like I always get what I want. I was never popular. People don't usually do what I want them to. Look at you—I want you to be attracted to me, but you walked out on our last date."

"I had a cold. I couldn't hear you very well. Like my sister Piper today," Phoebe said.

"Still, people don't usually react to me this way," he argued.

"How did you get the gig organizing the museum fund-raiser?" Phoebe asked. "That was a really high-profile event."

Daniel shrugged. "I went in and did a presentation like all the other event planners who were competing for the job. They picked me."

"Of course they did," Phoebe said.

"We don't always get the job. The company I work for is still new—a lot of times a more established company will get picked," Daniel said.

"But when you do the presentation, your company always gets the job," Phoebe said. "Right?"

He thought about it. "Well . . . yeah."

"At the museum gala, you weren't even that great at public speaking, no offense," Phoebe said. "You made the microphone shriek and hurt people's ears. But as soon as you started to talk, every bigwig in that place was completely enchanted with you."

Daniel still looked doubtful. "How come I'm so shy around women, then? If everybody loved me as much as you say, I should be like Casanova or somebody."

"Good point." Phoebe studied him. He was definitely a good-looking guy. But when he spoke, he seemed even more handsome. And he could say pretty much anything and still be attractive. "I think it's just because you're so sure that you don't know how to talk to women. You're so insecure about yourself that you don't even try. So they don't hear your voice."

"Then I was right to let Indar help me," Daniel said. "Otherwise I would never have even gotten a single date with you."

"Not true," Phoebe said. "All you had to do was ask."

Daniel leaned against the back of the bench and shook his head. "I still can't believe all this. You really think I have some kind of power—that I'm a witch?"

"Yes."

"I'm not sure I ever really believed all those stories about my mother's family," he said. "Not that I thought they were lying or anything. But I just figured that stuff was all in the past."

"Nope. You're a witch. Which means you have to make a choice," Phoebe told him. "Are you good or evil?"

"Well, I'm definitely not evil," he said in an offended tone.

"Then you'd better stop hanging out with a demon. Demons are evil," Phoebe told him. "Trust me."

"Not Indar."

Phoebe took Daniel's hand, ignoring his little nervous jump when she touched him. "Even Indar. We have to vanquish him, you know."

"No. You can't." Daniel turned toward her pleadingly. "I know it doesn't seem like things went very well between you and me, Phoebe, but believe me when I say it's the most success- ful I've ever been at dating. And that's all thanks to Indar. He gave me a game plan, so I would always know how to behave around you. It was really helpful."

"But—"

"Please," he said. "You can't hurt him. He's my friend."

Phoebe melted. How bad could the little demon be, anyway? "Okay," she promised Daniel. "We'll leave him alone."

"We will not leave him alone!" Paige cried. "He's a demon."

"But Daniel said they're friends," Phoebe argued, watching Paige whip up yet another batch of cold-vanquishing potion. "It's possible, you know. Not all demons are pure evil. Cole wasn't entirely evil."

"His demon half was," Piper said gently. Phoebe's ex-husband had been a unique case, and she knew it.

"It doesn't matter. Indar didn't seem like much of a threat," Phoebe said. "He hid behind Daniel. He didn't want to fight me."

"Maybe he didn't want to fight you right then. Maybe he has some other plan," Piper said.

"But . . ." Phoebe wanted to argue, but she couldn't think of anything to say.

"Face it, Phoebes. You got bamboozled by Daniel's voice again," Paige commented. "He said 'Don't kill the demon' and you thought that sounded totally logical."

Phoebe growled in frustration. Her sister was right. "We have to do a spell to counteract his voice," she decided. "I didn't get the impression that he was trying to put the whammy on me—I thought he just really likes Indar. But how can I know for sure? Anything he said would have seemed nice to me."

"So we still don't know where Daniel stands in all this," Piper commented. "It appears that he wasn't aware of his power or even of the fact that he's a witch."

"But he could be lying and we wouldn't know." Paige held up a bottle of potion. "Are you ready, Piper?"

"Whoa, hang on." Phoebe jumped up from the table. "If you're doing that spell again, I'm getting out of here. I don't want the cold to jump to me."

"Thanks for the vote of confidence." Paige frowned.

"No offense, sweetie, but that cold sucked. I'll just go up to my room while you do it."

"I think if you're in the house at all, you're fair game," Piper said.

"You guys, it's going to work," Paige insisted. "I changed the potion and now I've changed the spell. Trust me." She threw the potion at Piper's feet and said, "Bad health, disappear. Banished are you. Go away from here."

As the magic cloud dissipated, Piper took a deep breath and smiled. "Thank you."

"How long until it usually shows up in someone else?" Phoebe asked.

"A few hours," Piper told her. "Let's make the most of it."

"You guys!" Paige protested. "It will work."

"Sorry." Phoebe rubbed her sister's arm. "Okay, so what are we going to do about Daniel and Indar?"

"We can't do anything to hurt Daniel until we know for sure if he's good or bad," Piper said. "And I have a feeling that Leo and the Elders aren't going to be much help with that for a while."

"Not until Leo can get his new charge to stay out of danger for more than five minutes at a time," Paige agreed.

"Maybe we can figure it out on our own," Phoebe said. "But first we should make ourselves immune to Daniel's voice."

"And then we can set a trap." Piper glanced at Phoebe. "You have to keep dating Daniel."

"What? Why?" Phoebe cried.

"So we can find out what Indar's really up to. Or what Indar and Daniel are both up to together," Paige said. "Think about it: Indar has been using one witch, Daniel, to seduce another witch, you. There has to be a reason for that. Demons don't just meddle in the love lives of witches because they want us to be happy."

"Or else Daniel is a willing participant and they're trying to set you up," Piper added. "The only way to find out is to see what they do next. You keep dating Daniel, Indar keeps telling him what to do, and we see what happens."

"So I have to be bait," Phoebe said.

"Kind of," Paige admitted.

"But wait. How is that going to work now? Indar knows that I'm onto him," Phoebe said. "I caught him in Daniel's apartment. He watched Daniel talk me out of vanquishing him. If I keep dating Daniel, won't Indar assume that we're setting a trap for him?"

"He obviously knows about Daniel's voice. He'll think you're going along with whatever Daniel says," Piper replied. "You just have to act as if Daniel's voice is still working its voodoo."

"I can do that," Phoebe said. "I'll just agree with everything he says."

Paige handed Phoebe the phone. "Give him a call."

"No!" Piper cried, snatching it away. "We have to neutralize Daniel's voice first. Otherwise, Phoebe won't even have to pretend."

"Oops." Phoebe grabbed a pen and quickly wrote up a protection spell. Her sisters gathered around and they all recited:

Voice with power over actions,
Influences and attractions,
Have no sway on us henceforth.

"Now we're ready," Phoebe said, picking up the phone to call Daniel. "Let's do it."

Chapter 10

"I give up." Paige collapsed against the back of the couch and let out a groan. The signs were unmistakable—a scratchy throat, a stuffed-up nose, and a pounding headache. "How can it be? Why isn't the cold vanquished already?"

Piper handed her a decongestant pill and a glass of water. "And we thought demons were the toughest thing out there."

"What if it's me?" Paige moaned. "Maybe there's something wrong with my powers."

"Is anything else going wrong?" Piper asked.

"No," Paige admitted. "But it's the only option left. I know it's not the potion and it's not the spell. I'm the only other variable."

"Maybe you should just ride it out this time," Phoebe suggested, coming into the living room. "It's no good passing it around and around."

"You just don't want to be sick again," Paige mumbled.

"Did you talk to Daniel?" Piper asked Phoebe.

"Yup. I said I didn't mind if he still wanted advice from Indar. Since, you know, I'm kind of a romantic advisor myself." Phoebe grinned. "I said I figured everybody could use a little help in the love department."

"And he bought it?" Paige said.

"You bet. Not only that, but he told me exactly what Indar said to do next."

"What?" Piper asked.

"He thinks that Daniel needs to make a grand gesture in order to convince me that he's serious about me," Phoebe said. "So he wants to go away this weekend, to this little hotel in Tahoe. Daniel made reservations for us, but it's weird."

"It doesn't sound weird to me, it sounds nice," Piper grumbled. "You've been dating this guy for a couple of weeks and he's all about the romance. But I can't even get my husband to go out for a two-hour dinner."

"I heard that," Leo's voice said as white light filled the room. He orbed in and gave Piper a tired smile.

"Wow. Home before midnight," she said.

"Yeah. Poor Kerria is exhausted—I'm hoping it will keep her out of trouble for a while," Leo replied. "So what's going on?"

"Well, Daniel made reservations for us to go away this weekend," Phoebe said.

"Oh, no. I forgot to check on him." Leo ran

his hand through his hair, making it stand on end. "I'm sorry. But I guess if you're still going out with him, you must have decided that he's good."

"Nope," Phoebe said. "We're hoping this weekend date will help us figure that out. Then we can take care of the demon. The weird thing is that he wants us to go on Thursday night instead of Friday."

Paige scrunched up her face in confusion. "Is it cheaper or something?"

"I don't know, but he insisted," Phoebe said. "Even though it means I have to take a day off from work. I wanted to argue about it, but if his voice was still doing its magic on me I would think it was the greatest idea in the world. So I had to just say yes."

"Thursday?" Leo said. "Isn't that the thirtieth?"

"Yeah. Why?" Paige asked.

"It's a blue moon," Leo replied. "The second full moon this month."

"Girls' Day!" Piper and Phoebe cried together, laughing. Phoebe turned to Paige and Leo. "When we were little, Grams always said that it was a special Halliwell holiday if there was a blue moon," she explained. "We'd all spend the entire day cooking a big dinner and then we'd bring the food upstairs and have a picnic in the attic."

"I think it was all that cooking that made me grow up to be a chef," Piper added.

"Well, I didn't know about Girls' Day, and that's not what I was thinking. It can be a powerful moon, magically speaking," Leo said. "It's a day when bonds are broken."

"And that matters . . . why?" Piper asked.

"Kerria has made some enemies lately, and she'll be more vulnerable during that moon phase," he said. "I was hoping you and I could finally spend some time together, but I have a feeling she'll end up needing me."

"You're lucky I trust you or else I'd worry about this girl," Piper teased him.

"Why is she more vulnerable?" Paige croaked.

"Oh, just because unpredictable things can happen on a blue moon. If she hasn't fully embraced her powers, she could get separated from them on that day. I'll have to watch her carefully."

The baby monitor on the coffee table suddenly came to life with the sounds of Wyatt's cries. Piper moved to stand up. "I'll get him," Leo said quickly. "You've been doing all the work lately." He jogged off toward the stairs.

"See? That was romantic, kind of," Phoebe told Piper.

"I know. I shouldn't be mad at him. I'm just so frustrated. It shouldn't be this impossible to find time for romance," Piper said.

"Maybe you should call Indar for advice," Paige said. She chuckled at her own joke, but it immediately turned into a cough.

"You sound terrible," Phoebe told her.

"I know. I've tried everything, though. Medicine, herbs, magic . . . nothing gets rid of it for good."

"I guess what they say is true," Piper said.

"What?" Paige asked.

"There really is no cure for the common cold!"

"Hi, Aunt Paige!" Leo said in a funny voice, waving Wyatt's little hand at her as he carried his son into the kitchen on Wednesday morning.

"Hi, Wy-Wy," Paige replied, making a silly face to get the baby to laugh. "Don't come too close. I have the cold again," she told Leo.

"Still haven't found a way to vanquish it for good, huh?" he asked. He opened a cabinet and pulled out a jar of baby food for Wyatt.

"Nope. But it's okay," Paige said. "Though at first I was worried that my powers were to blame."

Leo's face fell. "I didn't even know that. I'm sorry, Paige. I've been a terrible husband lately, and I guess I've been a terrible Whitelighter, too. If you were worried about your powers, I should have been here to help."

Paige couldn't stand to see him so sad, even if he was maybe a little bit right about how he'd been acting lately. "We don't need you as much as Kerria does," Paige said, trying to make him feel better. "I've made my peace with the whole cold situation. It was my own fault."

"How?" Leo asked. He settled Wyatt into the high chair and began to feed him.

"I shouldn't have thought I could vanquish it," Paige said. "Everybody knows colds are impossible to get rid of."

Leo laughed. "I guess that's one way of looking at it."

"It's true. Just because I'm a witch doesn't mean I get to control everything," Paige said. "Think about it. Colds are part of nature. Why should I be able to vanquish nature? It's not like I'm all-powerful or anything."

"You didn't really think you were," Leo said.

"No, but still . . ." Paige took a sip of her lemon tea. "I got kind of carried away with having power. It's good to be able to help Innocents and fight evil, but I don't need to go around trying to fix everything that's wrong in the world. If I can vanquish a cold, why not cure cancer? Or AIDS?"

Leo swooped a spoonful of food through the air, pretending it was an airplane for Wyatt. "That's a pretty heavy realization," he told Paige.

"I know. All this thinking is making my headache even worse," Paige joked.

"Oh, no," Leo said, dropping the baby spoon with a clatter.

"I'm just kidding," Paige told him.

"No, it's Kerria," Leo said. "She's calling. She's in trouble again." He looked at Wyatt and sighed. "I promised Piper I'd take care of Wyatt this morning. I feel like I haven't seen him in weeks. Not when he's awake, anyway."

"Tell you what. I'll go see what Kerria needs," Paige offered. "I'm a Whitelighter in training. Maybe I can handle it."

Leo hesitated.

"Leo, seriously, let me take it," Paige insisted. "You need time with your son. And I promise I'll call you if it's anything too big."

"I shouldn't let you. . . ." His eyes went to Wyatt, who was reaching out for the bowl of food.

"Think of it as a scouting mission." Paige stood up. "I'll just find out what the problem is, then I'll come get you. At least you'll have time to finish feeding Wyatt. And, uh, when you're done you might want to go upstairs and give Piper a kiss or something. She's feeling neglected."

She gave him a little wave and orbed off to find Kerria.

"You're up early," Piper said, coming into the attic.

Phoebe glanced up from the Book of Shadows. She'd been flipping through it for the past ten minutes. "I'm looking for a description of our Girls' Day. Grams always made such a big deal of it that I thought she might have put an entry in here about it."

Piper's eyebrows drew together in concern. "What made you think about that?"

"It's just such a coincidence," Phoebe said. "I haven't thought about Girls' Day in years. I'd forgotten all about it."

"Me too," Piper admitted. "After we all left home, the whole thing just kind of fizzled."

"But don't you think it's weird that Daniel was so insistent on going away on the day of a blue moon?" Phoebe asked. "Especially when it's a magically important day, like Leo says."

"And especially if it was Indar's idea," Piper said. "Is there anything about it in there?"

Phoebe bent over the book. "There's a lot about moon phases in general, but I haven't gotten to blue moons yet."

Piper perched on one of the chairs scattered about the attic. "Girls' Day was always so much fun," she mused. "Remember? We got to stay home from school, and it was the one time Grams let us eat all the cookies and sweets we wanted."

"Except for Prue. She always wanted to gorge on potato chips instead," Phoebe said with a smile. She hadn't thought deeply about her childhood in a long time, but it was sweet to look back on it now, remembering their grandmother, who had raised them after their mom died. And their oldest sister, whom Phoebe had always looked up to when they were kids.

"It's funny, isn't it?" Piper said. "Grams had

us make a holiday of a blue moon, which is obviously a Wiccan thing, and she never even told us about the magic part of it."

"Well, she never told us about magic, period." Phoebe turned another page of the old book, and caught her breath. "Not when she was alive, anyway. But she's telling us about it now."

Piper jumped up and came over to join her. "What does it say?"

"'Blue moon—danger,'" Phoebe read.

"That doesn't sound good."

"'Traditionally a moon phase that loosens the bonds of magic, a blue moon could spell disaster for the Power of Three,'" Phoebe continued. "'While some witches may find the bonds between themselves and their powers lessened, the Charmed Ones will have an added worry. The ties that bind the three sisters together will also be loosened. It is imperative that the Power of Three be guarded on this day.'"

"Guarded how?" Piper asked.

"It seems as if Grams had a theory," Phoebe replied, scanning the rest of the page. "The Power of Three is always there, no matter where we are individually. But if we're not in the same place during a blue moon, the bonds that connect us are weak. Enemies can take advantage of that to sever the bonds completely—and destroy the Power of Three."

Piper let out a low whistle. "Wow. So that's what she was doing. Grams was making sure to protect the Power of Three, even before we knew anything about it."

"Girls' Day," Phoebe said. "She kept us together, all day, since the bonds between us would weaken if we were separated."

"You know what that means, don't you?" Piper asked. "Indar—and maybe Daniel—are trying to take advantage of the blue moon. That's why Daniel insisted on you going away with him on Thursday. He—or someone, anyway—wants to separate us."

Phoebe nodded grimly. "Looks like we'll all be going to Tahoe this weekend. It's the only way to keep us together."

"The question is, what are they planning?" Piper said thoughtfully. "It's possible that this is all an elaborate plot to get to Paige and me, not to you. If you're off with Daniel, then the Power of Three is weak and he can attack us here."

"Huh. So Indar might come here—and we'll all be in Tahoe." Phoebe chewed on her lip, thinking.

"Does that matter?" Piper asked. "We'll still be safe. And our main goal is to figure out where Daniel stands in all this. It's possible that he's just an Innocent, doing what Indar told him to do."

"How are we going to prove that, though?" Phoebe asked.

"Indar wants us to be weak. That means he's either going to try to kill us or steal our powers,"

Piper said. "If Daniel was in league with him, he'd be going after you while Indar went after Paige and me."

"So I go off on my romantic weekend with Daniel and wait to see whether he attacks me or not?" Phoebe asked.

"Hey, nobody said love was easy," Piper answered. "On the up side, if you make it through Thursday night with no attack, we'll know that Daniel isn't out to get you. Except romantically, of course."

"Somehow that isn't very comforting," Phoebe said. "A guy who's so shy that he trusts a demon to do his wooing for him?"

"Oh, come on." Piper grinned. "You've dated worse!"

Paige peered through the white light of her orbing to see a distraught-looking girl surrounded by three Tracer demons.

"Well, this doesn't look like fun," she said as she materialized at the girl's side.

The girl pushed her red bangs away from her eyes and stared at Paige. "Who are you?"

"Paige Matthews." Paige hurled a fireball at one demon and quickly orbed another demon into the fireball's path. Both demons went up in flames. The third one shimmered away immediately. Paige turned to the girl. "Kerria, I assume?"

"Yeah." Kerria looked shell-shocked. "What happened to them?"

"Well, two of them are dead and the other one took off. Tracer demons travel through dimensions, so he's probably somewhere in another dimension right now." Paige glanced around the room. "They trashed your place, huh?"

"No, actually that happened yesterday. I was fighting a warlock," Kerria said. "I haven't had time to clean up yet."

Paige let out a whistle. "You're a busy girl."

"I'm sorry, I must be confused," Kerria said. "Who are you? I called for my Whitelighter."

"Right. I'm his sister-in-law," Paige said. "I'm a Whitelighter too. Kind of. I'm just starting out."

"Well, you did a pretty amazing job," Kerria said. "I didn't know Whitelighters could throw fire."

"Oh, that. Most Whitelighters can't do that, actually. I'm half-witch." Paige searched the messy apartment for a box of tissues, grabbed one, and sneezed into it. "Sorry, I have a cold."

"Paige . . . you're one of the Charmed Ones!" Kerria cried. "Of course. No wonder you're so powerful. What are you doing here?"

"Leo's busy with another charge," Paige said. "His son. He hasn't been seeing much of his family lately, so I came instead."

Kerria looked ashamed. "That's because of me, isn't it?"

"Mostly," Paige said honestly.

"I know. I seem to keep getting in trouble."

Kerria cleared a space on the couch and gestured for Paige to sit. "I don't know why."

"How long have you had your powers?" Paige asked.

"Two months."

"Two months and you're already fighting with warlocks and being hunted by Tracer demons?" Paige cried. "You work fast."

"Really? That's not normal?"

"No," Paige said. "How did you get involved with all these bad guys?"

"Well, I found out that I was a witch and that I had all this power to help people," Kerria said. She plopped down on the floor and went into a yoga pose. "So I started going out and looking for people to help. It's incredible how many demons there are in this city."

"I know," Paige agreed. "But why are you out looking for them?"

Kerria stopped mid-stretch and stared at her. "What do you mean?"

"I mean why are you going after demons?" Paige asked. "And warlocks?"

"Because they're evil," Kerria said slowly, as if Paige were the stupidest person on Earth. "And they need to be vanquished."

"Yes," Paige said. "Evil is bad, all right. But it's not up to you to stamp it out single-handedly."

Kerria shook her head. "I don't understand."

"Look, Kerria. You're a new witch. You can't possibly have complete mastery over your powers yet," Paige said gently. "I'm still learning about my powers and I've had them for a lot longer than you."

"So?"

"So, you're not ready for warlocks and demons yet. Not this many of them, anyway," Paige told her. "Don't get me wrong, it's great that you want to fight evil. But getting yourself killed isn't going to help anybody. And dragging Leo here to help you day after day means that you're putting all his other charges in danger because he can't be there for them."

Kerria gasped. "I never thought about that."

"I know you didn't," Paige said. "But you have to start thinking that way. You have to start looking at the big picture. There's a lot of evil in the world, and one witch can't destroy it all. No matter what you do, you'll never get rid of everything bad in the world."

"I'm still supposed to try, though, aren't I?" Kerria asked.

"I don't think so," Paige replied. "I've been trying to get rid of this cold for a long time, and it keeps coming back. Magic has no effect on it. So I'm thinking that maybe magic isn't the answer to everything. Maybe there are some things that we just can't control, no matter what."

"But what does that have to do with demons?" Kerria asked.

"Nothing, really. What I meant is, all you can

control is yourself and your powers. You have to respect the limits of your power," Paige explained. "Take smaller steps. Fight what you're strong enough to fight. You can't solve all the world's problems, and nobody is expecting you to."

Kerria thought for a moment. "I have to say, that's a huge relief," she finally admitted. "Because ever since I got my powers, I thought I was supposed to be out there vanquishing every single bad guy I could find. And you know what?"

"What?" Paige asked.

"I'm exhausted!"

"Are you sure you don't want us to come with you?" Leo asked Piper on Thursday afternoon. He shifted Wyatt onto his left hip and went on. "Kerria promised me she wouldn't need me at all this weekend."

"That's great, honey, but I have to work now," Piper said as she tossed her overnight bag into the trunk of the car. "You know Paige and I have to stay close to Phoebe throughout the blue moon. I don't want to have to worry about Wyatt while we're trying to deal with Indar and Daniel."

"I know," Leo said. "I'd just like to spend some time with you while I have a chance. Who knows how long Kerria will leave me alone?"

"Don't worry about Kerria," Paige told him, throwing her own bag into the car. "She's not going to bother you too much anymore."

Leo's eyebrows shot up. "Why not?"

"She's decided to focus on honing her powers," Paige said. "She's not going to go out looking for trouble anymore."

"She said that?"

"Yup." Paige grinned at him. "You're welcome."

"Wait. How did you do that?" Leo asked. "I keep trying to protect her from all these demons she gets involved with, and she's never said anything about staying home and honing her powers."

"I just had a talk with her," Paige said. "You know, girl to girl. I told her she's not responsible for the whole world. And that she can't control it."

"Did she think she could?" Leo asked, astonished.

"Of course she did," Paige said. "She's a powerful woman. We all think we can control the world."

Piper laughed. "Right now I'll settle for controlling our schedule. Phoebe and Daniel should be leaving in ten minutes. We have to be behind them." She kissed Wyatt's chubby little cheek, then stood on tiptoe to kiss Leo good-bye.

"Hey, wait!" he called, following her around to the driver's side. "Be careful. Call me if you need me."

"I will," she promised.

"And Piper?"

"Hmm?"

"When you get back, will you have dinner with me?" Leo asked. "For our anniversary?"

Piper smiled. "I thought you'd never ask."

"I'm really looking forward to dinner tonight, Phoebe," Daniel said as he turned the car off of the main road and headed up into the hills near Tahoe. "The hotel has a five-star restaurant. I made reservations for us at the best table in the house—it looks right out over the lake. They guaranteed me that it would be the most romantic place in the room."

"Sounds great," Phoebe replied.

"I thought that afterward we could walk down to this little café on the shore. What do you think?" Daniel went on. "Moonlight on the water, some cappuccino, and I hear there's live piano music every night."

"Wow. Sounds . . . great," Phoebe repeated. She wasn't sure what else to say. The drive had been three hours long, but it felt like forever. Trying to have a regular conversation with Daniel had turned into a huge chore. She had to pretend that every word he said had a magical effect on her *and* she had to ignore the fact that all of those words had been written for him by a demon. Pretending that this was some kind of normal date with a normal guy seemed impossible.

"I'm so glad you came," Daniel said. "I know things have gotten a little strained between us, but I'm really hoping we can start over."

He reached for her hand and brought it to his lips. Phoebe forced a smile, thinking about how romantic that sentiment would be if only it were truly coming from Daniel rather than Indar.

"Especially now that you've opened my eyes to my, um, my true . . . identity. . . ."

"To the fact that you're a witch," Phoebe said.

"Yeah. It makes me feel closer to you," Daniel continued. "It's just one more thing we have in common."

Phoebe couldn't take it anymore. "Daniel, it's the *only* thing we have in common," she said as gently as she could. "At least as far as I know. You've never really told me anything else about yourself. On all of our dates, you only wanted to talk about me."

"I wanted to know all about you. You fascinate me," Daniel said. "I could listen to your stories forever."

Phoebe had to stop herself from rolling her eyes. Had lines like that really worked on her during their first few dates? Indar must have been counting on Daniel's voice to take care of everything for him.

"Did Indar tell you that women like to talk about themselves?" Phoebe asked.

Daniel gaped at her. "Uh . . ."

"It's okay," Phoebe said quickly. "I'd probably tell people the same thing—if you want to make someone like you, you have to make them feel special. And the best way to make someone feel special is to make them the center of attention. So get them to talk about themselves."

"Yeah. That's exactly what Indar said," Daniel admitted. "But that's not the only reason I did it. I really did want to know about you, Phoebe. You're . . . you're exotic. You're beautiful and mysterious and you're so self-confident. I wish I could be more confident, the way you are. I really wanted to know what makes you tick."

Phoebe felt a little flutter of pleased embarrassment. She got the feeling that it was Daniel talking right now, not Indar. But how could she be sure? "That's so sweet," she said.

"I mean it," Daniel told her.

"Did Indar tell you to say all that?" Phoebe couldn't help asking.

"No," Daniel insisted. "Not everything I do is because of him."

"So it was your idea to come up here tonight, on a Thursday?" Phoebe asked. "Not Indar's?"

Daniel didn't answer. Phoebe bit her lip, worried. Had she gone too far? If she were still under the power of Daniel's voice, she probably wouldn't be questioning him like this. And she had to make him think his voice was still working on her.

"I wanted to make sure we got the good reservations at the restaurant," Daniel finally said.

He's lying. Phoebe was sure of it. Until now, he'd sounded honest. But something in his voice

had changed. Which probably meant that the
trip up here on the night of the blue moon had
been Indar's idea. The only question left was
whether Daniel was in on the demon's plan or
not.

Phoebe casually glanced in the side mirror of
the car, checking to make sure that Piper and
Paige were still behind them. The Charmed
Ones didn't know how close together they had
to stay to protect the Power of Three during the
blue moon, but they'd all figured the closer, the
better. Grams had always made sure they were
in the same room. Piper had phoned ahead to
the hotel to make sure they could be put in the
room right next to Phoebe's.

When Daniel pulled up to the hotel, Paige
drove right past them in the driveway and
parked about thirty feet away. Phoebe knew her
sisters would wait until she and Daniel had
checked in before they went into the hotel themselves.

"I got us rooms that have a lake view from
one side and a mountain view from the other,"
Daniel told her as they followed the bellhop up
to the top floor of the exclusive hotel. "And your
room has a fireplace. I thought you might like
that."

"I love fireplaces. Thank you." Phoebe took
his hand, trying to act as if she were here for a
romantic weekend rather than a showdown
between good and evil.

The bellhop stopped at her room and put her suitcase on the stand. "I'm just going to freshen up after the drive," Phoebe said. "Then we can meet downstairs and go out to explore the town."

"Okay," Daniel replied. "I'm right next door if you need me."

Phoebe pulled out her cell the second the door closed behind him. She dialed Piper. "I'm upstairs, you guys can come in now," she said when her sister answered.

"We're on our way. Did you find out anything on the drive?" Piper asked. Phoebe heard Paige coughing in the background.

"No. I think whatever Indar is planning will probably go down tonight," Phoebe replied. "When the moon rises."

"I hope I did the right thing leaving Leo and Wyatt at home," Piper said, her voice worried. "If Indar really does attack there, they could be in danger. Who knows what he's really capable of?"

"Wyatt has his protective bubble, and Leo can take care of himself," Phoebe assured her. "Besides, when Indar finds out that you and Paige aren't there, he'll probably just take off. He's not after Wyatt."

"The truth is, we don't know what he's after," Piper said with a sigh. "Well, first things first. We have to find out if Daniel is on the demon's side or not."

"I think I'll go over and get him," Phoebe said. "I was supposed to meet him downstairs to

go out for a walk, but I don't want to risk running into you guys. I'll swing by his room and
convince him to leave by the door at the end of
the hall."

"All right. Paige and I will get settled into the
room on the other side of you," Piper said.
"Don't go too far. The three of us have to stay
close together."

"Don't worry. I'll pretend to twist my ankle or
something and come back in ten minutes."
Phoebe hung up the phone, quickly checked her
hair in the mirror, and hurried out into the hallway. The bellhop was just leaving Daniel's room.
"Oh, hold the door!" she called to him.

He stuck his hand out to keep Daniel's door
from closing, and Phoebe ran over to grab it.
"Thanks." As the bellhop headed off down the
hall, she turned and pushed open the door.
"Daniel?" she called. "It's me."

But it wasn't Daniel in the hotel room.

It was Indar.

Chapter 11

Phoebe gasped.

And the demon was gone.

"Phoebe?" Daniel rushed in through the sliding glass door that led to the balcony. "What's wrong?"

She stalked all the way into his room, her head swiveling right to left as she searched for Indar. She'd definitely seen him. He'd been standing right by the armoire. But now he was gone, and there was no sense of him anywhere.

"What are you looking for?" Daniel asked.

Phoebe turned to him accusingly. "Is Indar here?"

Daniel gaped at her. His mouth opened, but he didn't say anything. Fury filled Phoebe's body. She was so sick of feeling this way, not knowing whether Daniel was her enemy or an Innocent whom she should be protecting.

"Daniel?" she demanded. "I thought I just saw your demon friend. Is he here too?"

A dark red blush spread from Daniel's neck up to his forehead. "Um . . ."

"Where did he go?" Phoebe cried, spinning around. "Is he invisible?"

"He's not here," Daniel said. "He really isn't."

"Well, he was three seconds ago! I just saw him. Why was he here?" she cried. "Is he going to sit next to you at dinner and tell you what to say? Is that your idea of a romantic weekend?" She took a step closer. "Or do you have something else planned?"

Daniel backed away, his eyes wide with alarm. "What are you talking about?" he asked.

Phoebe realized that she was advancing on him as if she were about to attack. And Daniel did look truly confused. Phoebe did another scan of the room. No Indar. She forced herself to relax and took a step back.

"Sorry," she said. "I just wasn't expecting him to be here. I thought you and I were spending the weekend by ourselves, to really get to know each other."

"We are. We will," Daniel said in a rush. "Indar suggested this hotel, and he suggested that we get away, just the two of us. But that's all. He's not involved in any other way. I promise."

Phoebe studied his face. He was as cute as ever, and he looked sincere. She knew his power wasn't swaying her anymore. She wanted to believe he was an innocent guy being used by a demon. She wanted to believe him.

But she didn't.

"I thought you wanted to go to the café by the lake," Phoebe said on the way upstairs after dinner. "Isn't that why we skipped coffee?"

Daniel tugged at the collar of his dress shirt, loosening his tie. He glanced around the elevator as if he felt trapped. "Yeah," he said. "Uh, I think it's open until midnight, though. We can go later."

Phoebe narrowed her eyes at him. He was acting even stranger than usual. Ever since they'd finished eating, Daniel had been nervous. He'd entirely dropped the romantic act and he barely even seemed to notice that Phoebe was there. As soon as they'd paid the bill, he bolted for the elevator, saying he needed to get back to his room.

"Do you feel okay?" she asked.

Daniel's eyes lit up as if she'd given him a great idea. "No! I don't, no. I feel sick."

Phoebe didn't buy it. "What's wrong?"

"Um, I guess I ate something bad." Daniel made a face and grabbed his stomach. "That's why I want to go upstairs for a while."

She knew he was lying. But he obviously wanted to get up to their rooms. Was this part of his plan with Indar? She knew her sisters would be waiting upstairs if she needed them, but if he decided to attack her in the elevator, what could she do? She didn't even know for sure whether Indar was here in Tahoe or back in San Francisco looking for Piper and Paige. She'd tucked a bottle of vanquishing potion into her purse just in case. Whether or not Indar had really been in Daniel's room earlier, she wanted to be prepared for anything. Phoebe casually moved to sling her purse over her shoulder so her hands would be free for fighting if necessary.

The elevator came to a stop on the top floor with a gentle *ding*.

Phoebe braced herself as the door slid open. Would Indar be on the other side? Was she about to be attacked?

Daniel sprang from the elevator as soon as the doors stopped moving. "I'll call you later!" he said over his shoulder. Then he was gone, running for his room.

Phoebe stood in the hallway, openmouthed.

Daniel unlocked his door and disappeared inside the room without so much as a glance at her.

Slowly, she turned in a circle, checking out the hallway. Was Indar waiting out here to attack?

Nothing happened.

A door creaked open, and Paige stuck her head out. "What's going on?" she whispered.

"I have no clue." Phoebe went over to her door and slid the key card into the slot. "Maybe there's an ambush waiting for me inside." Her sisters came out of their room and got her back as she shoved her door open and jumped into the room, ready for a fight.

The room was empty. Everything was exactly as she'd left it.

"I don't get it," Piper said, closing the door behind them. "What's happening?"

Phoebe shrugged. "Daniel had this whole plan. Candlelight dinner followed by a stroll down to the lake to a little café with music and great views."

"I should have Indar give Leo a few tips," Piper murmured.

"I figured that if Daniel was going to attack, it would be on the walk to the lake," Phoebe said. "But instead he scrapped the whole thing and ran back to his room. He was barely even polite about it."

"Huh." Paige bounced on the edge of Phoebe's bed. "Do you think he got a call from Indar? Maybe the demon tried to attack the Manor and found out that we aren't there. He could've let Daniel know that the plans had changed."

Piper was shaking her head. "Leo would have orbed here if something had happened. Or Wyatt would have."

Phoebe pulled back the curtain and glanced up at the inky black sky. A perfect full moon was just rising over the treetops. "The blue moon is up," she said. "If Daniel and Indar have a plan to attack us, now should be the time. What gives?"

"Shh!" Paige said. "I heard something."

"What?" Phoebe asked.

"From next door. Daniel's room."

Phoebe listened. There were a few thumps, but she couldn't make out what he was doing. Luckily, she didn't have to. A movement outside the window caught her eye. Instinctively, Phoebe dropped the curtain back over most of the window. "Shut off the light," she hissed to her sisters.

Piper hit the switch, plunging the room into darkness.

Phoebe slowly drew back the curtain, letting the pale moonlight into the room. On the balcony next door, she could see a figure moving in the dim light. He paused and turned his head toward her window. Phoebe froze, hoping the glare of the moon on the window hid her from his sight. After a moment he turned away.

"It's Daniel," she whispered. "He's out on his balcony."

"Is he coming in here?" Piper asked.

Phoebe watched as he leaned over the railing of his balcony, peering down the three stories to the ground below. "I don't know," she said.

Daniel suddenly swung one leg over the railing and began climbing—but not toward Phoebe's balcony. "He's climbing down," Paige cried, looking over Phoebe's shoulder.

"Why?" Piper asked.

Phoebe and Paige both shrugged. Daniel had reached the balcony below his and was climbing over the side of that one. "He's going all the way to the bottom," Phoebe cried. "We have to go after him!"

"I'm not going that way," Paige said. "These jeans are not made for extreme hotel sports. And all this congestion in my head is messing with my balance."

Piper yanked open the door and they all ran out into the hallway. "Stairs!" Phoebe yelled, heading toward the end of the hall. They rushed down the three flights and pushed open the side door. It let them out in the dark corner of the parking lot. The cement backed up onto a pretty little forest with a few footpaths running through it for the hotel guests to hike on.

"He would have come down over there," Paige said, pointing to the back of the building. "Let's go."

"Okay, but quietly," Piper warned. "For all we know, this is a trap."

Paige sneezed.

They both glared at her. "Sorry," she muttered.

Phoebe led the way along the nearest path. It ran parallel to the back of the hotel, but at least it offered a little cover. When she reached the level of Daniel's room, she stopped. Paige silently pointed to the ground. Footsteps in the blanket of fallen leaves led from the hotel to the path they were on. It looked as if Daniel had gone ahead of them on the same path.

Moving as slowly and quietly as possible, Phoebe kept going. After twenty yards, the path veered away from the hotel and wound deeper into the woods. Up ahead, there was a dim light and the muted sound of voices.

Phoebe turned back to her sisters. "The path runs into a clearing," she whispered. "I think Daniel is up there. I'm going to see. You guys wait here."

Piper grabbed her arm. "What if he's waiting to ambush you?" she whispered.

"That's why you're waiting here," Phoebe replied. "If he grabs me, you can sneak up and freeze him." She turned and walked the rest of the way to the clearing. In the center were two rough-hewn wooden benches and a little fire pit. It was obviously meant to be a romantic spot, but what was going on there now was anything but romantic.

A fire burned in the pit, the flames streaked with purple and green. Daniel knelt on one side of it and Indar on the other side. He was chanting. As Phoebe approached, the fire climbed higher, its unnatural colors getting brighter and the smoke growing thicker.

This time Indar didn't vanish as soon as she looked at him. He was definitely there, and he was definitely working some kind of spell. Phoebe didn't hesitate. She rushed into the clearing.

"Stop!" she yelled.

Indar turned toward her, his eyes blazing yellow. He leaped to his feet—and stumbled backward, falling over one of the wooden benches.

"What's going on?" she demanded, looking at Daniel.

He smiled casually. "We're doing a spell. Don't tell me you don't know what that looks like. You're a witch."

She couldn't believe the change in him. Gone was the sweet, shy guy who couldn't even meet her eye without blushing. "I was right. You're not an Innocent," she spat. "You've been in league with this demon all along."

Daniel shrugged.

"Well, that's about to end." Phoebe pulled the bottle of vanquishing potion from her pocket. "You can't talk me out of vanquishing him now."

"Oh. Too bad," Daniel said mildly.

Indar clumsily got to his feet, staring at Daniel. He turned his yellow eyes to Phoebe just as she raised her arm to hurl the bottle at him.

"No!" he shrieked. He raced around the bench and tried to hide behind it.

"You really are the wimpiest demon I have ever seen," Phoebe muttered. She stepped closer, ready to throw the potion over the top of the bench.

"I'm not a demon!" he cried, his voice filled with terror. "I'm not Indar. I'm Daniel."

Chapter 12

Phoebe froze. "Huh?"

"I'm Daniel," the demon said. "Phoebe, it's me."

Phoebe turned to Daniel. "What's going on?"

Daniel just smiled and sat down on the other bench.

"Tell her it's me," the demon insisted, its voice high and thin. "Phoebe, believe me. We did a spell. We switched bodies."

Her mouth dropped open and she whirled around to Daniel. "You'd better be kidding." But the way he stared straight back at her—no blush—and the confident look in his eyes told her everything she needed to know. That might be Daniel's body, but it wasn't Daniel.

"Oh my God," she said, turning back to the little purple guy with the yellow eyes. "Daniel. What were you thinking?"

"I didn't expect . . . well, I don't know what I

expected," he said. "I can't figure out how to use this body," he complained.

"You'll get used to it," Indar said with Daniel's voice.

Phoebe shook her head. This made no sense. Body switching? Weren't they supposed to be attacking her? Or Piper and Paige?

"Wait a minute. You snuck out during our special 'starting over' weekend to go off and switch bodies with the guy who's supposed to be helping you?" Phoebe said. "Just for the record, fire him as your romantic advisor."

"We had a deal," Daniel replied. "I just didn't know it was supposed to happen tonight. I wasn't expecting to have to sneak out." He shuffled his scaly feet. "Even I know that's not the way to a woman's heart."

"The timing was important. I had no choice," Indar said smoothly. "We would have been done already if Phoebe hadn't interrupted us."

"Done?" Phoebe looked back and forth between them. "Done with what?"

Neither of them answered.

"You said you had a deal. What deal?" Phoebe asked. She stood in front of Daniel, forcing him to raise his yellow eyes to her face. "Daniel, what deal?"

"Indar said he'd teach me how to talk to you and get you to go out with me," Daniel said. "And in return he needed my help to do a spell."

"A body-switching spell? And that seemed

like a good idea to you?" Phoebe cried.

"No, no, no," Indar said. Phoebe couldn't help staring at him. It was too weird to see Daniel's body and hear Daniel's voice . . . but know that it wasn't Daniel. "There's a very special spell that I need to do, and it has to be done tonight. But I couldn't do it in my demon form. I have to be human in order for it to work."

"He just needed to borrow my body for a few minutes to do a spell," Daniel said. "It seemed like a small price to pay if I got to be with you in return."

Phoebe sighed. "Daniel, that's probably the most romantic thing you've said to me since we met," she told him. "It's also the stupidest. You made a deal to give your body to a demon! That's just . . . just insane."

"He said it wouldn't hurt, and it didn't," Daniel said. "I'm fine. I feel a little weird, but I'm fine."

"There's a demon possessing your body," Phoebe pointed out.

"You don't understand. Indar needs my help just like I needed his," Daniel told her. "He has to do a love spell. He's trying to get his true love to return to him."

Phoebe rolled her eyes. "Why would you need a human body in order to do a love spell?" she asked Indar. "There's no rule about that."

"Are you sure?" he asked.

"Yes." She crossed her arms over her chest

and waited. Indar chewed on his lip, clearly trying to come up with some excuse.

"Wait, there's no rule?" Daniel asked in his creepy demon voice. "Of course there's a rule. Indar told me all about it. His true love is human so he needs to be human too."

"Right," Indar said. "Only while I do the spell. It's an apples and oranges thing. I can't do it as a demon unless my love is also a demon."

"But once you do the spell as a human, she's going to love you even in your demon form?" Phoebe asked skeptically.

"Exactly." He smiled widely. "You're as smart as Daniel said you were. I'm so glad the two of you are working things out."

Phoebe felt a wave of revulsion wash over her as she realized what Indar was doing. He was trying to use Daniel's powerful voice to sway her. She opened her mouth to tell him that it wouldn't work, then closed it again. Whatever Indar's real plan was, she knew it had nothing to do with a love spell. The best way to find out was to let him go through with it.

She glanced around the clearing. The fire had gone back to normal now that the body-switching spell was over. It crackled and burned with a cheerful orange glow. Unfortunately, the flames were also lower, which plunged the forest around them into deeper blackness. She couldn't see her sisters anywhere.

"Why should I trust you?" she asked, raising

her voice so Piper and Paige could hear if they were nearby. "You're a demon."

"I keep telling you, he's a good demon," Daniel said. "He's just unlucky in love. All he wants is to be happy with the woman of his dreams."

"It's true," Indar agreed. "Besides, you're very powerful, Phoebe. Daniel told me that you're a witch. So you must know that I'm no threat to you. Look at me." He gestured to Daniel, who sat curled into a small purple ball on the bench. "I'm puny. I'm a coward. I have no powers except for defensive ones. My only talent is disappearing when I'm in danger."

"And talking," Daniel put in. "Don't sell yourself short. You know how to speak to women. It's a power I wish I had."

Phoebe had to stifle a groan. Poor, sweet Daniel still didn't get it. All he had to do to seduce anyone in the world was open his mouth. His magical voice took care of everything else. But he kept on thinking that Indar had helped him in some way. Her doubts about him vanished—he really was an Innocent in all this. He truly thought Indar was his friend, and more than that, that this devious demon was a good guy.

She had to protect Daniel—from Indar *and* from his own naïveté.

"Please, Phoebe, let Indar do his love spell," Daniel pleaded. "He held up his end of the deal—he taught me how to talk to you. I know things haven't been perfect, but I've been able to spend time with you and that's enough. I owe him this."

Phoebe looked around again. She still couldn't see Paige or Piper, but she knew they were out there in the woods. If she needed help, they'd come.

"Okay," she said loudly. "Do your spell." She sat down next to Daniel. If Indar tried to do anything to him, she'd have to protect him. But she had a feeling that it wasn't Daniel that the demon was really after.

Indar leaped off the bench and raised his arms to the sky. His eyes flashed with excitement as he loudly chanted his spell:

> *Blue moon that loosens the ties,*
> *Send great magic across the skies.*
> *Power of Three, come to me!*

Triumphant, Indar turned to Phoebe. "Now I have your power, witch!" he crowed. "And your sisters'. And Daniel's."

Daniel started. "What did you do? That wasn't a love spell! How dare you attack Phoebe and her family?"

Indar laughed. "You're so pathetic," he said. "You still don't understand. I have your body. I have your power. And now I have the Power of Three as well. I'm unstoppable! I'm the strongest witch who ever lived—and it's all thanks to you, you miserable little creature. You belong in that body. You're just as cowardly and useless as it is."

Daniel's yellow eyes went wide as the truth finally sank in. Phoebe felt him stiffen in horror beside her, and she was afraid he might faint.

"Time to deal with you, witch." Indar raised his arms and glared at Phoebe. "Ever wonder how it feels to be hit by a fireball?" he asked. "Or maybe I should freeze you instead? Or should I use the powers differently—maybe orb your head off your body? I bet that kind of thing never even occurred to your sister."

"Well, no. But that's just because I'm not a psychopath," Paige said, stepping out of the woods.

Indar jumped in surprise.

"You should try it, though," Piper added, coming out of the darkness on the other side of the clearing. "Let's see if you really have all those powers you think you have."

Indar's eyes darted between them, filled with doubt. Phoebe stepped up to close the gap between her sisters. "Did you really think we'd let the Power of Three be broken today?" she asked.

"The blue moon made you vulnerable," Indar bellowed. But his voice held doubt.

"Then go ahead. Freeze me," Phoebe dared him. "Throw a fireball. Do it."

Eyes blazing with hatred, Indar raised his arm and swung it at Phoebe. She forced herself not to flinch.

Nothing happened.

Phoebe felt relief rush though her. He didn't have Paige's power. Grams had been right—as long as they were together, the Power of Three was safe.

Indar roared in frustration and hurled his arm forward again.

Nothing happened. Again.

"Your technique is all wrong." Paige stepped up, trapping Indar between herself and Piper. "Let me show you how it's done."

She raised her arm to throw a fireball at him, which everyone knew would kill him once and for all.

But Daniel let out a shriek of terror. "No!" he screamed. "You can't vanquish him—he's still in my body!"

Chapter 13

"Paige, stop!" Phoebe cried.

Paige hesitated. Indar took advantage of the confusion and bolted, speeding through the trees and back toward the hotel.

Piper quickly threw up her hands and froze him in midstride. "Okay. What's going on?" she asked. "We could see you from the trees and we heard some of what you said, but we didn't get the whole story." She frowned at Daniel. "What's with Shorty here?"

"This is Daniel," Phoebe explained. "He and Indar did a spell to switch their bodies."

"So they *are* in cahoots," Paige said. "Why did you stop me from vanquishing him, then? Shouldn't we vanquish them both?"

"No. And we can't hurt Daniel's body," Phoebe said. "Daniel is an Innocent. I'm sure of it. He didn't know what he was getting into."

"I thought it was temporary," Daniel said

miserably. "Indar said he was only going to borrow my body to do a love spell."

"And you believed him?" Paige snorted.

"I guess I have a lot to learn about all this magic stuff," Daniel replied. "Aren't there any good demons?"

"Not really," Phoebe told him. "That's why they're called *demons*."

"I can't believe I'm such an idiot," he mumbled. "I've ruined everything."

"Daniel, you have to focus," Piper said. "We need to vanquish Indar, which means we need to get you back into your body and him back into his. Do you remember the spell he used to do the body switch?"

"No. I didn't pay much attention," Daniel said. "I just wanted to hurry up and get it all over with so I could go back and take Phoebe to the lakeside café. Indar said it would only take a few minutes."

"Yeah, two minutes for him to steal your body, two minutes for him to steal our powers," Paige said. "That's all he needed."

"It would have been a good plan," Phoebe commented. "The powers of four witches combined in one person."

"Lucky you three were smart enough to figure it out," Daniel said. "I just handed over my power. Not to mention my body."

"We've had a lot more practice," Paige told him. "You'll learn."

"Is there some kind of generic spell to do a body switch?" Piper asked. She glanced over at Indar, who was just beginning to move. He got one step farther away before Piper froze him again.

"I have no idea," Phoebe said. "How are we supposed to find out?"

White light filled the clearing as Leo orbed in with Wyatt in his arms. When he saw Daniel in Indar's body, he immediately tightened his grip on the baby.

"It's okay, this is our Innocent," Piper said. She reached over for Wyatt. "What are you two doing here?"

"I was just putting Wyatt to bed when there was a magic wind," Leo said. "It blew through the Manor and kind of petered out. I figured I'd better check on you guys."

"You mean you came for us?" Piper asked. "To help us?"

"I am your Whitelighter. I'll always be there for you if you need me," Leo replied. He peered at Daniel and the frozen Indar. "Everything under control?"

"That depends," Piper said. "Do you know anything about body switching?"

"I have to get my body back," Daniel put in. "I'm starting to feel claustrophobic in here."

Leo frowned. "It's a complicated thing to do. The spells are notoriously unreliable. I'm actually kind of surprised that Indar managed it."

"He really isn't a very powerful demon," Phoebe said. "It's odd that he could pull it off."

"Blue moon," Paige said. "Magical bonds are weakened, remember? Our bonds to one another. Daniel's bond to his body."

"Plus Daniel was a willing participant," Piper said. "So there wasn't any obstacle to overcome."

"That's the key, I'm afraid." Leo frowned. "We've still got the blue moon—Indar's bond to the body will be weak. But he'll fight to keep Daniel's body. I don't know how we're supposed to get him out of it, even with a spell."

"I guess he won't fall for the old 'I just want to borrow it' trick, huh?" Phoebe asked.

"Not unless he's as dumb as me," Daniel said. "If only he'd gotten my gullible personality along with my body."

"If only he *hadn't* gotten your magical voice along with your body," Phoebe said. "Then you could just talk him into reversing the spell."

"That's easy enough," Leo answered. "We'll just get the voice power back."

They all stared at him.

"Excuse me?" Phoebe asked.

"The voice is Daniel's power, right?" Leo asked.

"Yeah," Paige said. "Why?"

"The power belongs to its owner," Leo replied. "If you steal someone's body, it's just their body. Not their soul. The power belongs with the soul."

"But Indar has Daniel's voice. I heard it," Phoebe said.

"And I have his," Daniel said in the demon's scratchy tones.

"Did Indar say anything about your powers in his body-switching spell?" Leo asked.

Daniel shook his scaly head. "I would have remembered that. I would've thought it was weird because he was only supposed to use my body temporarily."

"I'd say your voices switched just because you didn't know any better," Leo guessed. "If you girls do the basic spell to call a witch's power, it should return to Daniel with no problem."

"And then what?" Piper asked, refreezing Indar as he started to move again.

"Then it's up to Daniel," Phoebe said, turning to him.

"Wh-what?" Daniel croaked.

"If you hadn't been in such denial all along about being a witch, none of this would have happened," Phoebe told him. "That power is yours. It belongs to you. And you're going to have to use it."

"But I don't know how," he protested. "I'm still having trouble believing in it. I know you keep telling me I'm powerful, but I can't even have a normal conversation with you, Phoebe."

She took Daniel's claw in her hand and looked him straight in the eye. "That's not true. You and I have had a lot of conversations, and you do just fine on your own. Indar didn't give you any help at all. In fact, all the talking you've done with me for the past week has been just you, without even the benefit of your power."

"What do you mean?"

"We did a spell to make sure your voice had no effect on us," Piper put in. "We couldn't let you keep on swaying us when we didn't know if you were good or evil."

Daniel managed to look hurt, even with the ugly face of a demon. "You thought I was evil?"

"We couldn't be sure," Phoebe told him. "You kept talking me out of vanquishing a demon, after all."

"So all this weekend . . . all through dinner tonight and the drive up here . . . my voice had no power on you?"

"None," Phoebe said. "And you did fine."

"Indar told me what to say," Daniel said glumly. "He even wrote out things for me to memorize."

"Daniel, this may shock you, but I could tell when it was you talking and when it was Indar," Phoebe said. "And I definitely preferred talking to just you."

He gazed at her, his eyes filled with astonishment.

Paige cleared her throat. "Uh, sorry to interrupt, but we've got a frozen demon in Daniel's body and we still don't know what we're doing about it."

"Right. Sorry. Listen, Daniel," Phoebe said seriously. "We're going to get your power back for you. But after that, you're on your own. You gave your body to a demon and it's up to you to get it back."

"But how?"

"You'll have to figure it out," she told him. "Your power is strong, and if you embrace it, you should be able to talk Indar into doing whatever you want him to. But you're going to have to believe in yourself. Otherwise it won't work."

"Are we ready for the spell?" Piper asked, handing Wyatt back to Leo.

Phoebe nodded and walked over to join her sisters near the fire. Together, they recited:

Powers of the witches rise
Course unseen across the skies.
Come to us who call you near;
Come to us and settle here.

The fire leaped up in the pit, sending blue flames into the sky as a smell like honeysuckle filled the air. Indar unfroze and ran for a few steps before he gave a little choking sound and stumbled to his knees. At the same time, Daniel grabbed his throat as if he couldn't breathe. His yellow eyes went wide with alarm.

"This doesn't look good," Paige murmured.

Phoebe reached out for Daniel—and he suddenly relaxed. On the other side of the clearing, Indar collapsed to the ground.

"I think it worked," Daniel said. The voice was deep and resonant, the powerful voice that Phoebe had first heard at the museum gala.

Indar sat up on the pathway, confused. "What happened?" he asked in the demon's thin, reedy tones.

"We took Daniel's power back," Phoebe told him. "And now you're going to give him his body back, too."

Indar climbed to his feet. "I don't think so. At least I'm getting something out of this deal. See you later, loser," he called to Daniel. Then he turned and sauntered away down the path.

Piper raised her hands to freeze him.

"No!" Paige and Leo cried at the same time.

"Daniel needs to take care of this for himself," Paige said.

Daniel looked panicked.

"Stop him," Phoebe coached him.

"Stop," Daniel squeaked, his voice cracking.

Indar stopped.

Phoebe held her breath. *Is he responding to Daniel's power?* she wondered. Was it possible that Daniel's voice had strong enough magic to overcome his complete lack of confidence?

Indar spun around and stalked toward Daniel, Daniel's blue eyes blazing in his angry face, and Daniel's handsome features twisted into a sneer of disgust.

I guess not, Phoebe thought.

Daniel, in Indar's body, stumbled backward, trying to get away.

Indar backed him up to one of the wooden benches, trapping him against it. Daniel's tall, thin body towered over the little purple body of the demon. Terrified, Daniel sank down onto the bench.

"What are you going to do, Daniel? Fight me for your body?" Indar demanded. "I know what you can do in that body, remember? Nothing. Just run and hide. Or disappear."

"You can't keep my body," Daniel whimpered. "It's not fair."

"Oh, wait a minute," Indar went on in a mocking tone. "You don't even know how to make yourself disappear, do you?"

"This isn't going well," Piper murmured.

Phoebe twisted her hands together. Why was Daniel just sitting there and taking all this? Why didn't he stand up for himself?

"Guess you'll make an even lamer demon than I did," Indar said, shaking his head at Daniel. "So long."

He turned around and stopped, looking Phoebe up and down. "Aren't you going to help your little boyfriend?"

"No," Phoebe said. "He doesn't need my help. He's stronger than you on his own."

"You wish." Indar pushed past her and headed for the pathway.

Phoebe whirled around and glared at Daniel. "Do something!" she snapped. "That jerk is walking away with your body. With your life! Are you just going to let him?"

"I don't know what to do," Daniel cried. "It's not like I can just ask him for my body back."

"Why not?" Phoebe demanded. "When we were at the mall, didn't everyone do what you wanted?"

"That's different."

"You're right. This is much more important," Phoebe said. "Daniel, you want to be the shy, nice guy who nobody notices. Well, you're not and you never have been. You're a powerful witch. You can't escape that. Now *use your power.*"

"Indar is almost gone," Paige said nervously. "We can't let him get away—we have to vanquish him."

"No," Daniel cried. "You can't hurt my body."

"Then stop him," Phoebe said. "It's up to you."

"Stop," Daniel called.

Indar ignored him.

"I said stop!" Daniel yelled. "Now!"

Indar stopped.

Daniel's eyebrows shot up in surprise. "Get back here with my body," he said, his voice growing more confident.

Indar turned around, moving in a jerky manner as if he were fighting his own muscles.

"I want my body back," Daniel told him.

"No," Indar said through gritted teeth.

"You lied to me," Daniel said. "You claimed to be my friend. You made a deal with me, but it was all a lie. You never intended to give my body back, and the only reason you wanted to see me with Phoebe was because you wanted to attack her and her family. You're evil."

Indar was listening, enthralled by Daniel's magical voice. Phoebe could see confusion in his eyes. She knew exactly how he felt—he wanted to fight with Daniel, but he couldn't. He wanted to think Daniel was wrong, but he couldn't.

Daniel's power was working.

"I was nice enough to lend you my body," Daniel went on. "And now I want it back."

There was a long pause. Then Indar nodded. "Okay."

Phoebe let go of a breath she didn't even know she'd been holding. Daniel glanced over at her. "What now?" he asked.

"Um, we need to know what spell he used," she replied.

"Indar, I want you to do the spell again, the same one you used before to switch our bodies," Daniel said.

"Okay," Indar answered. He knelt on one side of the fire and gestured for Daniel to kneel on the opposite side.

> *Powers of earth,*
> *Hear my call.*
> *What's mine is yours,*
> *What's yours is mine.*
> *You become me,*
> *Switch it all.*

The flames in the fire pit became streaked with purple and green as he chanted, the smoke growing thicker and the colors brighter until he finished speaking.

Daniel and Indar both fell backward, looking slightly stunned.

"Daniel?" Phoebe asked.

Daniel's body turned toward her, his blue eyes meeting hers. "Yes."

"Is it really you?" she asked.

"It's me." His voice was deep and rich, back to normal. But he was holding eye contact with her, and Daniel never did that.

"No, *I'm* Daniel," said the purple demon in a thin, reedy voice. "He's lying. Again."

"Oh, great," Piper groaned. "How are we supposed to know who to believe?"

"I hate snow peas," the one in Daniel's body said, still staring right into Phoebe's eyes. "My favorite color is bright yellow. My favorite movie is *Titanic*. And my favorite breed of dog is the Labradoodle."

"Um, am I missing something?" Paige murmured. "Did their brains get scrambled?"

But Phoebe felt a huge smile spreading across her face. "No. Daniel's just telling me a little something about himself for a change."

"And this is the first time I've managed to actually look at you for more than five seconds without having a meltdown," Daniel added. "Without the 'help' of Indar, that is."

Phoebe laughed. She went over and threw her arms around his neck. "Welcome back."

"Thanks." He hugged her close. "Thank you for having faith in me."

"Well, that was before I knew your favorite movie is *Titanic*," she joked.

"You guys, Indar just disappeared," Paige cried.

"What? Where did he go?" Piper looked frantically around the clearing.

Phoebe groaned. "His only powers are defensive powers," she said. "Whenever there's danger, he disappears. You can't even sense him."

"Indar! Show yourself," Daniel called in a commanding tone. "Right now!"

Indar appeared at the edge of the woods, two feet behind Leo and Wyatt.

"Stay there," Daniel told him. "No moving, no disappearing."

Indar stayed.

"Thanks," Piper said. "That's a pretty nifty power."

"I'm starting to think so too." Daniel grinned.

"Let's vanquish this guy and get out of here," Phoebe suggested. She pulled the bottle of vanquishing potion out of her pocket and got ready to throw it.

"Wait!" Paige yelled. She pulled out a different bottle of potion and hurled it at her own feet. "Bad health, disappear. Banished are you. Go away, now, from here."

A mist rose around her head. Paige took a deep breath—and smiled. "I feel so much better now. How do you feel, Indar?"

Indar sneezed. Then he sneezed again.

"Okay, vanquish him," Paige said.

Phoebe threw the potion, and Indar vanished in a puff of lavender smoke.

He was gone.

Chapter 14

"I thought maybe we could go to Absinthe, that restaurant you wanted to try," Daniel said a few days later.

"I doubt they're still holding my reservation," Phoebe joked. She steered Daniel away from a couple of teenage girls who had started following them through the park. Whenever he said so much as "excuse me" or "thank you" to someone, chances were good that they would follow him for blocks.

Daniel seemed oblivious to it. He was completely focused on Phoebe. "I know I acted really rude about it, especially since you had reservations and everything," he said. "I had a whole evening of pizza-making planned with topics of conversation and everything. I'd practiced it all with Indar. I couldn't face the idea of trying to improvise."

"And now?" Phoebe asked. She sat down on

a wrought-iron bench, and Daniel sat next to her.

"Honestly? I'm still pretty intimidated by you," he admitted. "I know you keep saying that I'm not making a fool of myself, but I feel like I am."

"You're not. Trust me. You're an incredibly sweet guy and nothing you say is stupid or embarrassing." Phoebe took a deep breath. "But . . ."

"But?" Daniel winced. "'But' is never good. Indar told me that, and I think he was right."

"Yeah," she said. "I'm sorry. You're a great guy, but I can't go out with you."

Daniel stared down at his feet. "You don't like me anymore because you did that spell to make my voice powerless on you."

"That's not it," she said. "Although yes, it was probably your power that kept me dating you for as long as I did. But that's not the reason."

"Then what is?" he asked.

"Daniel, you've just found out a huge thing about yourself," she said gently. "You need time to focus on the fact that you're a witch. You have power, and that means accountability. You don't even notice it, but everybody you talk to falls under your sway. That's a lot of influence to have over people, and you have to learn to use it responsibly." She nudged him in the arm. "You can't go around sweet-talking every man, woman, and animal that you meet!"

"I'm not doing it on purpose," he protested.

"I know. That's the problem." Phoebe smiled at him. "You're going to be a terrific witch. You've already helped vanquish one demon, and you'll be a strong force for good in the world."

"You have more confidence in me than I have in myself," he said glumly. "And now I can't see you anymore."

"That's exactly the point," she said. "You need to be confident on your own. A witch who doesn't trust himself is a witch who's vulnerable to creatures like Indar."

Daniel sighed. "I still think you're the most fascinating woman on the planet. Just for the record."

"See? You don't even need that voice power of yours," Phoebe said with a sad smile. "You're a charmer all by yourself." She kissed him on the cheek and stood up. "Good-bye, Daniel."

"Hey, lady. Lookin' good," Phoebe said when she walked in the front door. Piper was putting on lipstick in the hall mirror, looking amazing in a deep purple dress and stiletto heels.

"Thanks. I even bought a new outfit for the occasion," Piper said.

"It's not every day you get to celebrate your wedding anniversary," Leo added. He came up behind Piper and slipped his arms around her waist.

"Two weeks late," Piper added.

Phoebe laughed. "I'm glad you guys are finally getting a chance to have a little romance."

"Thanks to Paige's words of wisdom," Leo said.

"I won't let it go to my head," Paige joked. She came out of the kitchen carrying Wyatt in her arms. "I'm just glad I could talk some sense into Kerria."

"The Elders were so impressed with Paige that they've assigned her her own charge," Leo told Phoebe.

"Yup. Say hello to the Whitelighter assigned to a new witch," Paige said. "Daniel Lemond."

Phoebe gasped. "You're Daniel's Whitelighter?"

"I am." Paige grinned. "I'm really looking forward to it. You know, I really think Daniel's going to be a great witch once he learns to embrace his power. He just needs a little more self-confidence."

"I'll say," Phoebe agreed. "Though I think he's starting to come around."

"And who knows?" Paige said. "Give me a few months with him, and maybe he really will be the perfect man for you, Phoebes. For real this time!"